©2001 Torunn Momtazi

Per Petterson is the author of five novels, including *In the Wake* and *To Siberia*. *Out Stealing Horses* has won the IMPAC Dublin Literary Award, the Independent Foreign Fiction Prize, and the Norwegian Booksellers' Prize. A former librarian and bookseller, Petterson lives in Oslo, Norway.

Out Stealing Horses

Additional Praise for *Out Stealing Horses*

"Much like a Raymond Carver short story, Petterson's narrative takes its time, and much of the prose, especially describing the Norwegian landscape and the hard labor of living in it, is hypnotic and grimly detailed."
—*The Boston Globe*

"A remarkable novel . . . as touching and enthralling as any more traditional novel, its qualities enhanced by the candor and simplicity of Per Petterson's style and Anne Born's limpid English translation."
—*The Spectator* (UK)

"Petterson's writing is accessible and intelligent. . . . [The] imagistic intensity and the shadowy treatment of character make *Out Stealing Horses* feel more like a long short story than a novel. That's not necessarily a problem, as the story's heartbreak and evocation of the natural world are reminiscent of Hemingway's Nick Adams stories."
—*Houston Chronicle*

"Petterson's spare and deliberate prose has astonishing force, and the narrative gains further power from the artful interplay of Trond's childhood and adult perspectives. Loss is conveyed with all the intensity of a boy's perception, but acquires new resonance in the brooding consciousness of the older man."   —*The New Yorker*

"Wonderful . . . Petterson captures perfectly the flavor of adolescence. . . . [He] accepts with great tenderness the way his characters respond to fate, and the varied nature of their resilience is what makes the novel, in the end, so moving."   —*The Seattle Times*

"A masterpiece of tough romance . . . *Out Stealing Horses* is one of my favorite two or three new novels to appear this year."   —*The New York Sun*

"Not merely a luminous story of the turning-points that waymark the end of childhood, but a genuine work of art."   —*The Independent* (UK)

"Petterson fluently jumbles his chronology, sustaining mysteries within several subplots and vivifying ever-green ideas about determinism and the bonds of family. But the real trick is in the way everything finally, neatly converges into an emotional jolt."
                                    —*Entertainment Weekly* (Grade: A)

"Haunting, minimalist prose and expert pacing give this quiet story from Norway native Petterson an undeniably authoritative presence."   —*Kirkus Reviews*

"A minor masterpiece of death and delusion in a Nordic land."   —*The Guardian* (UK)

"A marvelous book."   —*The Philadelphia Inquirer*

"Extraordinary."   —*Baltimore Sun*

"Wonderful . . . Petterson accepts with great tenderness the way his characters respond to fate, and the varied nature of their resilience is what makes the novel, in the end, so moving."   —*The Plain Dealer* (Cleveland)

Out
Stealing
Horses

Per Petterson

Translated by Anne Born

PICADOR

NEW YORK

www.picadorusa.com

Picador® is a U.S. registered trademark and is used by St. Martin's Press under license from Pan Books Limited.

For information on Picador Reading Group Guides, please contact Picador. E-mail: readinggroupguides@picadorusa.com

The sentences that form the first paragraph on page 221, repeated in part on page 224, are the opening lines of Jean Rhys's novel *Voyage in the Dark*. (Constable 1934, Penguin Books 1969, 2000). © Jean Rhys, 1934.

A Lannan Translation Selection
Funding the translation and publication of exceptional literary works

ISBN-13: 978-0-312-42708-5
ISBN-10: 0-312-42708-5

Originally published in Norway by Forlaget Oktober, with the title *Ut og stjæle hester*

First published in the United States by Graywolf Press

10 9 8 7

Out Stealing Horses

I

I

EARLY NOVEMBER. It's nine o'clock. The titmice are banging against the window. Sometimes they fly dizzily off after the impact, other times they fall and lie struggling in the new snow until they can take off again. I don't know what they want that I have. I look out the window at the forest. There is a reddish light over the trees by the lake. It is starting to blow. I can see the shape of the wind on the water.

I live here now, in a small house in the far east of Norway. A river flows into the lake. It is not much of a river, and it gets shallow in the summer, but in the spring and autumn it runs briskly, and there *are* trout in it. I have caught some myself. The mouth of the river is only a hundred metres from here. I can just see it from my kitchen window once the birch leaves have fallen. As now in November. There is a cottage down by the river that I can see when its lights are on if I go out onto my doorstep. A man lives there. He is older than I am, I think. Or he seems to be. But perhaps that's because I do not realise what I look like myself, or life has been tougher for him than it has been for me. I cannot rule that out. He has a dog, a border collie.

I have a bird table on a pole a little way out in my

yard. When it is getting light in the morning I sit at the kitchen table with a cup of coffee and watch them come fluttering in. I have seen eight different species so far, which is more than anywhere else I have lived, but only the titmice fly into the window. I have lived in many places. Now I am here. When the light comes I have been awake for several hours. Stoked the fire. Walked around, read yesterday's paper, washed yesterday's dishes, there were not many. Listened to the B.B.C. I keep the radio on most of the day. I listen to the news, cannot break that habit, but I do not know what to make of it any more. They say sixty-seven is no age, not nowadays, and it does not feel it either, I feel pretty spry. But when I listen to the news it no longer has the same place in my life. It does not affect my view of the world as once it did. Maybe there is something wrong with the news, the way it is reported, maybe there's too much of it. The good thing about the B.B.C.'s World Service, which is broadcast early in the morning, is that everything sounds foreign, that nothing is said about Norway, and that I can get updated on the position of countries like Jamaica, Pakistan, India and Sri Lanka in a sport such as cricket; a game I have never seen played and never will see, if I have a say in the matter. But what I have noticed is that 'The Motherland', England, is constantly being beaten. That's always something.

I too have a dog. Her name is Lyra. What breed she is would not be easy to say. It's not that important. We have been out already, with a torch, on the path we usually take, along the lake with its few millimetres of ice up against the bank where the dead rushes are yellow with autumn, and the snow fell silently, heavily out of the dark sky above, making Lyra sneeze with delight. Now she lies there close to the stove, asleep. It has stopped snowing. As the day wears on it will all melt. I can tell that from the thermometer. The red column is rising with the sun.

All my life I have longed to be alone in a place like this. Even when everything was going well, as it often did. I can say that much. That it often did. I have been lucky. But even then, for instance in the middle of an embrace and someone whispering words in my ear I wanted to hear, I could suddenly get a longing to be in a place where there was only silence. Years might go by and I did not think about it, but that does not mean that I did not long to be there. And now I am here, and it is almost exactly as I had imagined it.

In less than two months' time this millennium will be finished. There will be festivities and fireworks in the parish I am a part of. I shall not go near any of that. I will stay at home with Lyra, perhaps go for a walk down to the lake to see if the ice will carry my weight. I am guessing minus ten and moonlight, and then I will stoke the fire, put a record on the old gramophone with Billie Holiday's voice almost a whisper, like when I heard her in the Oslo Colosseum some time in the 50s, almost burned out, yet still magic, and then fittingly get drunk on a bottle I have standing by in the cupboard. When the record ends I will go to bed and sleep as heavily as it is possible to sleep without being dead, and awake to a new millennium and not let it mean a thing. I am looking forward to that.

In the meantime, I am spending my days getting this place in order. There is quite a lot that needs doing, I did not pay much for it. In fact, I had been prepared to shell out a lot more to lay my hands on the house and the grounds, but there was not much competition. I do understand why now, but it doesn't matter. I am pleased anyway. I try to do most of the work myself, even though I could have paid a carpenter, I am far from skint, but then it would have gone too fast. I want to use the time it takes. Time is important to me now, I tell myself. Not that it should pass quickly or slowly, but be only *time*, be something I live inside and fill with physical things and activities that I can divide it up by, so that it grows distinct to me and does not vanish when I am not looking.

Something happened last night.

I had gone to bed in the small room beside the kitchen where I put a temporary bed up under the window, and I had fallen asleep, it was past midnight, and it was pitch dark outside. Going out for a last pee behind the house I could feel the cold. I give myself that liberty. For the time being there is nothing but an outdoor toilet here. No one can see anyway, the forest standing thick to the west.

What woke me was a loud, penetrating sound repeated at brief intervals, followed by silence, and then starting again. I sat up in bed, opened the window a crack and looked out. Through the darkness I could see the yellow beam of a torch a little way down the road by the river. The person holding the torch must be the one making the sound I had heard, but I couldn't understand what kind of sound it was or why he was making it. If it *was* a he. Then the ray of light swung aimlessly to right and left, as if resigned, and I caught a glimpse of the lined face of my neighbour. He had something in his mouth that looked like a cigar, and then the sound came again, and I realised it was a dog whistle, although I had never seen one before. And he started to call the dog. Poker, he shouted, Poker, which was the dog's name. Come here, boy, he shouted, and I lay down in bed again and closed my eyes, but I knew I would not get back to sleep.

All I wanted was to sleep. I have grown fussy about the hours I get, and although they are not many, I need them in a completely different way than before. A ruined night throws a dark shadow for many days ahead and makes me irritable and feel out of place. I have no time for that. I need to concentrate. All the same, I sat up in bed again, swung my legs in the pitch black to the floor and found my clothes over the back of the chair. I had to gasp when I felt how cold they were. Then I went through the kitchen and into the hall and pulled on my old pea jacket, took the torch from the shelf and went out onto the steps. It was coal black. I opened the door again, put my hand in and switched on the outside light. That helped. The red-painted outhouse wall threw a warm glow across the yard.

I have been lucky, I say to myself. I can go out to a neighbour in the night when he is searching for his dog, and it will take me only a couple of days and I will be OK again. I switched on the torch and began walking down the road from the yard towards where he was still standing on the gentle slope, swinging his torch so that the beam moved slowly round in a circle towards the edge of the forest, across the road, along the river bank and back to its starting point. Poker, he called, Poker, and then blew the whistle, and the sound had an unpleasantly high frequency in the quiet of the night, and his face, his body, were hidden in the darkness. I did not know him, had only spoken to him a few times on the way past his cottage when I was out with Lyra most often at quite an early

hour, and I suddenly felt like going back in again and for-
getting all about it; what could I do anyway, but now he
must have seen the light of my torch, and it was too late,
and after all there was something about this character I
could barely make out there in the night alone. He ought
not to be alone like that. It was not right.

'Hello,' I called quietly, mindful of the silence. He
turned, and for a moment I could not see anything, the
beam of his torch hit me straight in my face, and when he
realised that, he aimed the torch down. I stood still for a
few seconds to recover my night vision, then I walked to
where he was, and we stood there together, each with our
bright beam pointing from hip height at the landscape
around us, and nothing resembled what it looked like by
day. I have grown accustomed to the dark. I cannot remember ever being afraid of it, but I must have been,
and now it feels natural and safe and transparent—no
matter how much in fact is hidden there, though that
means nothing. Nothing can challenge the lightness and
freedom of the body; height unconfined, distance unlim-
ited, for these are not the properties of darkness. It is only
an immeasurable space to move about inside.

'He's run off again,' said my neighbour. 'Poker. My
dog, that is. It happens. He always comes back. But it's
hard to sleep when he's gone like that. There are wolves
in the forest now. At the same time, I feel I can't keep the
door shut.'

He seems a bit embarrassed. I probably would be if it
were *my* dog. I don't know what I would do if Lyra had
run off, whether I would go out by myself to search for
her.

'Did you know that they say the border collie is the most intelligent dog in the world?' he said.

'I have heard that,' I said.

'He is smarter than I am, Poker, and he knows it.' My neighbour shook his head. 'He's about to take charge, I'm afraid.'

'Well, that's not so good,' I said.

'No,' he said.

It struck me that we had never really introduced ourselves, so I raised my hand, shining the torch on it so he could see it and said:

'Trond Sander.' That confused him. It took him a moment or two to change his torch to his left hand and take my right hand with his, and then he said:

'Lars. Lars Haug. With a g.'

'How do you do?' I said, and it sounded as bizarre and strange out there in the dark night as when my father said 'Condolences' at a funeral in the depths of the forest many, many years ago, and immediately I regretted saying those four words, but Lars Haug did not seem to notice. Maybe he thought it was the proper thing to say, and that the situation was no odder than it might be whenever grown men greet each other in a field.

There was silence all around us. There had been days and nights of rain and wind and incessant roaring in the pines and the spruce, but now there was absolute stillness in the forest, not a shadow moving, and we stood still, my neighbour and I, staring into the dark, then I felt certain there was something behind me. I could not escape the sudden feeling of sheer cold down my back, and Lars Haug felt it too; he directed his torchlight at a point a couple of metres past me, and I turned, and there stood Poker, quite stiff and on guard. I have seen that before, how a dog can both sense and show the feeling of guilt, and like most of us it was something it did not like, especially when its owner started talking to it in an almost childlike tone of voice, which did not go well with the weather-beaten, lined face of a man who had undoubtedly been out on a cold night before and dealt with wayward things, complicated things in a contrary wind, things of high gravity—I could tell that when we shook hands.

'Ah, where have you been, Poker, you stupid dog, been disobedient to your daddy again? Shame on you, bad boy, shame on you, that's no way to behave,' and he took a step towards the dog, and it started growling deep down in its throat, flattening its ears. Lars Haug stopped in his tracks. He let his torch sink until it shone directly on the ground, and I could just pick out the white patches of the dog's coat, the black ones blending with the night, and it all looked strangely at odds and unsymmetrical as the growl low in the animal's throat went on from a slightly less definite point, and my neighbour said:

'I have shot a dog once before, and I promised myself then that I would never do it again. But now I don't know.' He had lost his confidence, it was clear, he could not work out his next move, and I suddenly felt desperately sorry for him. The feeling welled up from I don't know where, from some place out in the dark, where something might have happened in a different time entirely, or from somewhere in my own life I had long since forgotten, and it made me embarrassed and ill at ease. I cleared my throat and in a voice I could not wholly control I said:

'What kind of dog was it that you had to shoot?'

Although I do not think that that was what I was interested in, I had to say something to calm the sudden trembling in my chest.

'An Alsatian. But it was not mine. It happened on the farm where I grew up. My mother saw it first. It ran around at the edge of the forest hunting roe deer: two terrified young fauns we had several times seen from the window grazing in the brushwood at the edge of the north meadow. They always kept close, and they did so then. The Alsatian chased them, encircled them, bit at their hocks, and they were exhausted and didn't stand a chance. My mother could not bear to look any longer, so she phoned the bailiff and asked him what to do, and he said: 'You'll just have to shoot it.'

'That's a job for you, Lars,' she said when she had put the receiver down. 'Do you think you can manage it?' I didn't want to, I must say, I hardly ever touched that gun, but I felt really sorry for the fauns, and I couldn't exactly ask *her* to do it, and there was no-one else at home. My big brother was away at sea, and my step-father was in the forest felling timber for the neighbouring farmer as he usually did at that time of year. So I fetched the gun and walked across the meadow towards the forest. When I got there I couldn't see the dog anywhere. I stood still listening. It was autumn, the air was really clear in the middle of the day, and the quietness was almost uncanny. I turned and looked back to the house, where I knew my mother was by the window watching everything I did. She was not going to let me off. I looked into the forest again, along a path, and there suddenly I saw the two roe deer running in my direction. I knelt down and raised the gun and laid my cheek to the barrel, and the big fauns were so frantic with terror that they did not notice me, or they had not the strength to worry about yet another enemy. They did not change course at all, but ran straight at me and rushed past a hand's breadth from my shoulder, I heard them panting and saw the whites of their wide staring eyes.'

Lars Haug paused, raised the torch and shone it on Poker, who had not moved from his place just behind me. I did not turn, but I heard the dog's low growl. It was a disturbing sound, and the man in front of me bit his lip and ran the fingers of his left hand over his forehead with an uncertain movement before he went on.

'Thirty metres after them came the Alsatian. It was a huge beast. I fired immediately. I am sure I hit it, but it did not change speed or direction, a shudder might have run through its body, I really don't know, so I fired again, and it went down on its knees and got up again and kept on running. I was quite desperate and let off a third round, it was just a few metres from me, and it somersaulted and fell with its legs in the air and slid right up to the toes of my boots. But it was not dead. It lay there paralysed, looking straight up at me, and I felt sorry for it then, I must say, so I bent down to give it a last pat on the head, and it growled and snapped at my hand. I jumped back. It made me furious and I gave it two more rounds right through the head.'

Lars Haug stood there with his face barely visible, the torch hanging tiredly from his hand, throwing only a small yellow disc of light on the ground. Pine needles. Pebbles. Two fir-cones. Poker stood dead still without a sound, and I wondered whether dogs can hold their breath.

'Bloody hell,' I said.

'I was just eighteen,' he said. 'It's long ago, but I shall never forget it.'

'Then I can well understand why you will never shoot a dog again,' I said.

'We'll see about that,' said Lars Haug. 'But now I'd better take this one inside. It is late. Come, Poker,' he said, his voice sharp now, and started to walk down the road. Poker followed him obediently, some metres behind. When they came to the little bridge, Lars Haug stopped and waved his torch.

'Thank you for the company,' he said through the darkness. I waved my torch and turned to walk up the gentle slope to the house and opened the door and went into the lighted hall. For some reason I locked the door behind me, something I have not done since I moved out here. I did not like doing it, but all the same I did. I undressed and lay down in bed under the duvet staring at the ceiling waiting for the warmth to come. I felt a bit foolish. Then I closed my eyes. At some point while I was asleep it started to snow, and I am sure I was aware of it, in my sleep, that the weather changed and grew colder, and I knew I feared the winter, and I feared the snow if there was too much of it, and the fact that I had put myself in an impossible position, moving here. So then I dreamt fiercely about summer and it was still in my head when I woke up. I could have dreamt of any summer at all, but I did not, it turned out to be a very special summer, and I still think of it now when I sit at the kitchen table watching the light spread above the trees by the lake. Nothing looks as it did last night, and I cannot think of a single reason for locking the door. I am tired, but not as tired as I expected to be. I will last until evening, I know I will. I get up from the table, a little stiff, that back is not what it used to be, and Lyra, by the stove, raises her head and looks at me. Are we going out again? We are not, not yet. I have enough to do, thinking about this summer, which begins to trouble me. And that it has not done for many years.

2

WE WERE GOING OUT STEALING HORSES. That was what he said, standing at the door to the cabin where I was spending the summer with my father. I was fifteen. It was 1948 and one of the first days of July. Three years earlier the Germans had left, but I can't remember that we talked about them any longer. At least my father did not. He never said anything about the war.

Jon came often to our door, at all hours, wanting me to go out with him: shooting hares, walking through the forest in the pale moonlight right up to the top of the ridge when it was perfectly quiet, fishing for trout in the river, balancing on the shining yellow logs that still sailed the current close to our cabin long after the clearing of the river was done. It was risky, but I never said no and never said anything to my father about what we were up to. We could see a stretch of the river from the kitchen window, but it was not there that we did our balancing acts. We always started further down, nearly a kilometre, and sometimes we went so far and so fast on the logs that it took us an hour to walk back through the forest when at last we had scrambled onto the bank, soaking wet and shivering.

Jon wanted no company but mine. He had two younger brothers, the twins Lars and Odd, but he and I were the same age. I do not know who he was with for the rest of the year, when I was in Oslo. He never talked about that, and I never told him what I did in the city.

He never knocked, just came quietly up the path from

the river where his little boat was tied up, and waited at the door until I became aware that he was there. It never took long. Even in the morning early when I was still asleep, I might feel a restlessness far into my dream, as if I needed to pee and struggled to wake up before it was too late, and then when I opened my eyes and knew it wasn't *that*, I went directly to the door and opened it, and there he was. He smiled his little smile and squinted as he always did.

'Are you coming?' he said. 'We're going out stealing horses.'

It turned out that *we* meant only him and me as usual, and if I had not gone with him he would have gone alone, and that would have been no fun. Besides, it was hard to steal horses alone. Impossible, in fact.

'Have you been waiting long?' I said.

'I just got here.'

That's what he always said, and I never knew if it was true. I stood on the doorstep in only my underpants and looked over his shoulder. It was already light. There were wisps of mist on the river, and it was a little cold. It would soon warm up, but now I felt goose pimples spread over my thighs and stomach. Yet I stood there looking down to the river, watching it coming from round the bend a little further up, shining and soft from under the mist, and flow past. I knew it by heart. I had dreamt about it all winter.

'Which horses?' I said.

'Barkald's horses. He keeps them in the paddock in the forest, behind the farm.'

'I know. Come inside while I get dressed.'

'I'll wait here,' he said.

He never would come inside, maybe because of my

father. He never spoke to my father. Never said hello to him. Just looked down when they passed each other on the way to the shop. Then my father would stop and turn round to look at him and say:

'Wasn't that Jon?'

'Yes,' I said.

'What's wrong with him?' said my father every time, as if embarrassed, and each time I said:

'I don't know.'

And in fact I did not, and I never thought to ask. Now Jon stood on the doorstep that was only a flag-stone, gazing down at the river while I fetched my clothes from the back of one of the tree-trunk chairs, and pulled them on as quickly as I could. I did not like him having to stand there waiting, even though the door was open so he could see me the whole time.

Clearly I ought to have understood there was something special about that July morning, something to do with the fog on the river and the mist over the ridge perhaps, something about the white light in the sky, something in the way Jon said what he had to say or the way he moved or stood there stock still at the door. But I was only fifteen, and the only thing I noticed was that he did not carry the gun he always had with him in case a hare should cross our path, and that was not so strange, it would only have been in the way rustling horses. We weren't going to shoot the horses, after all. As far as I could see, he was the same as he always was: calm and intense at one and the same time with his eyes squinting, concentrating on what we were going to do, with no sign of impatience. That suited me well, for it was no secret that compared with him I was

a slowcoach in most of our exploits. He had years of train-
ing behind him. The only thing I was good at was riding
logs down the river, I had a built-in balance, a natural tal-
ent, Jon thought, though that was not how he would have
put it.

What he had taught me was to be reckless, taught me
that if I let myself go, did not slow myself down by thinking so much beforehand I could achieve many things I
would never have dreamt possible.

'OK. Ready, steady, go,' I said.

We set off together down the path to the river. It was
very early. The sun came gliding over the ridge with its fan
of light and gave to everything a brand-new colour, and
what was left of the fog above the water melted and disappeared. I felt the instant warmth through my sweater
and closed my eyes and walked on without once missing
my footing until I knew we had got to the bank. Then I
opened my eyes and clambered down the stream-washed
boulders and into the stern of the little boat. Jon pushed
off and jumped in, picked up the oars and rowed with
short, hard strokes straight into the stream, let the boat
drift a stretch and rowed again until we reached the opposite shore about fifty metres further down. Far enough for
the boat not to be seen from the cottage.

Then we climbed up the slope, Jon first with me at
his heels, and walked along the barbed wire fence by the
meadow where the grass stood tall under a light veil of
mist, and would soon be mowed and hung on racks to
dry in the sun. It was like walking up to your hips in
water, with no resistance, as in a dream. I often dreamt
about water then, I was friends with water.

It was Barkald's field, and we had come this way many

times, up between the fields to the road that led to the
shop, to buy magazines or sweets or other things we
had the money for; one øre, two øre and sometimes five
øre coins jingling in our pockets every step we took, or
we went to Jon's house in the other direction where his
mother greeted us so enthusiastically when we walked in
you would have thought I was the Crown Prince or something, and his father dived into the local paper or vanished out to the barn on some errand that just could not
wait. There was something there I did not understand. But
it did not worry me. He could stay in the barn as far as I
was concerned. I didn't give a damn. Whatever happened,
I was going home at summer's end.

Barkald's farm was on the far side of the road behind
some fields where he grew oats and barley every other
year, close up to the forest with the barn at an angle,
and in the forest he kept four horses in a large area he
had fenced in with barbed wire, from tree to tree at two
heights. It was his forest, and there was a lot of it. He
was the biggest landowner in the district. Neither of us
could stand the man, but I am not sure why. He had never
done anything to us or uttered an unfriendly word that
I had ever heard. But he had a big farm, and Jon was the
son of a smallholder. Almost everyone was a smallholder
alongside the river in this valley only a few kilometres
from the Swedish border, and most of them still lived off
the produce of their farms and the milk they delivered to
the dairy, and as lumberjacks in the logging season, for
Barkald in his forest, or elsewhere, and in the one owned
by a rich bastard from Bærum; thousands and thousands
of parcels of land to the north and the west. There wasn't
much money about, as far as I could make out. Maybe

Barkald had some, but Jon's father had none, and *my* father certainly did not have any, not that I knew about, anyhow. So how he had scraped together enough to buy the cabin where we stayed that summer is still a mystery. Frankly, I never had a clear idea what my father did to earn a living; to keep his life going, and mine, among others, because it often seemed to change from one thing to another, but there were always numerous tools involved, and small machines, and sometimes a great deal of planning and thinking with pencil in hand and journeys to all kinds of places around the country, places where I had never been and never knew what they looked like, but he was no longer on any other man's payroll. Often he had a great deal to do, at other times less, but still, he had managed to save enough money, and when we went there for the first time the year before, he walked round looking things over and smiling a secret smile and patting the trees, and sitting on a big stone on the river bank, his chin in his hand, looking out over the water as if he were among old friends. But of course it could not have been so: could it?

Jon and I left the meadow path and walked down the road, and although we had been this way many times before it was different now. We were out stealing horses and we knew it showed. We were criminals. That changes people, it changes something in their faces and gives them a particular way of walking no-one can do anything about. And stealing horses, that was the worst thing of all. We knew about the law west of Pecos, we had read the cowboy magazines, and although maybe we could say that we were *east* of Pecos, it was so far east that you might just as well say it the other way round, as it depended on which way you chose to look at the world, but with that law there was no mercy. If you were caught, it was straight up in a tree with a rope round your neck; rough hemp against the tender flesh, someone whacked the horse on its rump and it flew out from under your legs, and then you ran for your life in bottomless air while that very life flashed past in review with fainter and fainter images until they were empty of your own self and of all you had seen, and then filled with fog, and finally turned black. Just fifteen, was your last thought, that wasn't much, and all for a horse, and then everything was too late. Barkald's house sat heavy and grey at the edge of the forest, and it seemed more threatening than ever. The windows were dark so early in the morning, but maybe he was standing there looking down the road and could see the way we were walking and *knew*.

But it was too late to turn round now. We walked stiff-legged a couple of hundred metres down the gravel road, until the house disappeared round a bend, then up another path across another field that was Barkald's too, and into the forest. At first the wood was thick and dark among the spruce trunks with no underbrush at all, only deep green moss like a huge carpet that was soft to walk on, for the light never wholly found its way in here, and we walked along the path one in front of the other and felt it yield each time we put a foot down. Jon first with me at his heels on worn gym shoes. Then we turned off in a curve, still to the right, the space and the light above us gradually expanding until suddenly we saw the two strands of barbed wire glinting, and we were there. We looked in at a clearing where all the spruce had been felled and the sapling pine and birch trees were standing strangely tall and solitary with no shelter at their backs, and some of them had not survived the wind from the north and had fallen full length with their roots in the air. Between the spruce stumps the grass was growing lush and thick, and behind some bushes further on we saw the horses, only their rumps visible, tails swishing horse flies. We smelled the horse droppings and the wet boggy moss and the sweet, sharp, all-pervading odour of something greater than ourselves and beyond our comprehension; of the forest, which just went on and on to the north and into Sweden and over to Finland and further on the whole way to Siberia, and you could get lost in this forest and a hundred people go searching for weeks without a chance of finding you, and why should that be so bad, I wondered, to get lost here? But I did not know then how serious that thought was.

Jon bent down and crawled between the two rows of barbed wire with his hand pressing down on the lower one, and I lay on the ground and rolled underneath the lower one, and we came through without a tear in either trousers or sweaters. We got warily to our feet and walked through the grass towards the horses.

'That birch over there,' said Jon, pointing. 'Climb into it.' A big birch tree stood apart, not far from the horses, with strong branches, the lowest of them three metres off the ground. Without hesitation I walked softly over to the tree. The horses raised their heads and turned them towards me as I approached, but they stayed where they were, still munching, without shifting. Jon walked around them in a semicircle from the other side. I kicked off my shoes, put both hands behind the birch and found a firm foothold in a crack in the bark, then placed my other foot flat against the trunk, and so climbed up monkey-wise until I could get my left hand around the branch, and I leaned over and took hold with my right hand and let my feet slide off the rough trunk, and then I hung by my hands for a moment before hoisting myself up, and sat there with feet dangling. I could do things like that in those days.

'OK,' I called quietly. 'Ready.'

Jon squatted in front of the horses and talked to them in a low voice, and they stood quite still with their heads towards him and their ears pushed forward, listening to what was almost a whisper. Anyway, I could not hear what he said from where I sat on the branch, but when I had called 'OK' he sprang up, shouting:

'Hoi!' and stretched out his arms, and the horses wheeled round and started to run. Not very fast, but not very slow either, and two stampeded to the left and two came straight for my tree.

'Be prepared,' Jon called and shot three fingers up in the air in a boy scout salute.

'Always prepared,' I called back, twisted around with my stomach against the branch, kept my balance with my hands and opened my legs in the air like a pair of scissors. I felt a faint drumming in my chest from the hooves on the ground and up through the tree and a trembling from a quite different place, from inside myself, and it started in the stomach and settled in my hips. But it couldn't be helped so I did not think about it. I was ready.

And then the horses were there. I heard their hard breathing, and the vibration in the tree grew stronger, and the sound of the hooves filled my head, and when I could just about see the muzzle of the nearest one beneath me, I slid off the branch with my legs stiffly to the sides, and I let go and landed on the horse's back a bit too close to its neck, and its shoulder bones hit me in the crotch and sent a jet of nausea up into my throat. It looked so simple when Zorro did it in the film, but now tears began to flow, and I had to be sick and at the same time keep a firm hold of the mane with both hands, and I bent forwards and pressed my lips tight shut. The horse tossed its head wildly and its back beat against my crotch, and it accelerated into a full gallop, and the other horse followed suit, and together we thundered off among the tree trunks. I heard Jon yell 'Yahoo!' behind me and I felt like yelling too, but I couldn't do it, my mouth was so full of sick that I could not breathe, and then I let it pour onto the neck under me. Now there was a faint smell of sick and a lot of horse, and I could not hear Jon's voice any more. There was a rushing sound, and the hoof beats died down, and the horse's back drummed through my body like the beating of my heart, and then there was a sudden silence around me that spread over everything, and through that silence I heard the birds. I distinctly heard the blackbird from the top of a spruce tree, and clear as glass I heard the lark high up and several other birds whose song I did not know, and it was so weird, it was like a film without sound with another sound added, I was in two places at once, and nothing hurt.

'Yahoo!' I screamed, and could hear my own voice, but it seemed to be coming from a different place, from the great space where the birds sang, a bird's cry from inside that silence, and for a moment I was completely happy. My chest swelled up like an accordion's bellows, and each time I breathed there were notes coming out. And then I saw something sparkle through the trees in front of me, it was the barbed wire, we had galloped right across the clearing and were approaching the fence on the other side at great speed, and the horse's back beat hard against my crotch again, and I clung hard to the mane and thought: We're going to jump. But we did not jump. Just before the fence both horses turned sharply and the laws of physics tore me from my horse's back and sent me kicking and flailing on in a straight line through the air and right over the fence. I felt the wire tear at the sleeve of my sweater and a smarting pain, and then I was lying in the heather, and the impact knocked the air out of my body.

I think I was unconscious for a few seconds, because I remember I opened my eyes as if to a new beginning; nothing I saw was familiar to me, my head was empty, no thoughts, everything quite clean and the sky transparently blue, and I didn't know what I was called or even recognise my own body. Unnamed, I floated around looking at the world for the first time and felt it strangely illuminated and glassily beautiful, and then I heard a whinny and the thundering of hooves, and it all came back like a whirring boomerang and hit me on the forehead with a crack, and I thought, shit, I'm paralysed. I looked down at my bare feet sticking out of the heather, and they had no connection with me.

I was still lying there flat out when I saw Jon on horseback with a rope round the horse's muzzle come up to the fence. With the rope he could control it. He stopped just on the other side by pulling the rope, and the horse halted almost sideways to the fence. He looked down at me.

'Lying there, are you?' he said.

'I am paralysed,' I said.

'I don't think so,' he said.

'Maybe not,' I said. I looked down at my feet again. And then I stood up. It hurt, in my back and along one side, but nothing inside was damaged. Blood was running from a cut on my forearm and out through the sweater, which had a big tear in it just there, but that was all. I tore off what was left of the sleeve and tied it round the wounded arm. It smarted good and hard. Jon sat there calmly on his horse. Now I saw that he held my shoes in one hand.

'Are you going to get on again?' he said.

'I don't think so,' I said. 'My arse hurts,' although that was not where it hurt the most, and I thought Jon smiled a bit, but I was not sure, because the sun was in my face. He slid off his horse and loosened the rope round its muzzle, then sent it off with a wave of his hand. It was happy to leave.

Jon came out through the fence the same way he had gone in; light on his feet, not a scratch anywhere. He came over to me and dropped my shoes in the heather.

'Can you walk?' he said.

'I think so,' I said. I pushed my feet into the shoes without tying the knots, so as to avoid bending down, and then we walked on into the forest. Jon first with me at his heels with a tender crotch, my back stiff, one leg dragging slightly and one arm held firmly against my body, still further in among the trees, and I thought perhaps I might not manage to walk all the way back when the time came. And then I thought of my father's asking me to cut the grass behind the cabin a week ago. The grass had grown much too tall and would soon just bend down and stiffen to a withered mat nothing could grow up through. I could use the short scythe, he said, which was easier in the hand for an amateur. I fetched the scythe from the shed and set about it with all my strength, trying to move the way my father moved when I had seen him do what I was doing now, and I worked until I was suitably sweaty, and it really went pretty well even if the scythe was a tool completely new to me. But alongside the cabin wall there was a big patch of stinging nettles, growing tall and thick, and I worked my way around them in a wide arc, and then my father came round the house and stood looking at me. He held his head aslant and rubbed his chin, and I straightened up and waited to hear what he would say.

'Why not cut down the nettles?' he said.

I looked down at the short scythe handle and across at the tall nettles.

'It will hurt,' I said. Then he looked at me with half a smile and a little shake of the head.

'You decide for yourself when it will hurt,' he said, suddenly getting serious. He walked over to the nettles and took hold of the smarting plants with his bare hands and began to pull them up with perfect calm, one after the other, throwing them into a heap, and he did not stop before he had pulled them all up. Nothing in his face indicated that it hurt, and I felt a bit ashamed as I walked along the path after Jon, and I straightened up and changed gait and walked as I normally would, and after only a few steps I could not think why I had not done so at once.

'Where are we going?' I said.

'There is something I want to show you,' he said. 'It's not far.'

The sun was high in the sky now, it was hot under the trees, it smelt hot, and from everywhere in the forest around us there were sounds; of beating wings, of branches bending and twigs breaking, and the scream of a hawk and a hare's last sigh, and the tiny muffled boom each time a bee hit a flower. I heard the ants crawling in the heather, and the path we followed rose with the hillside; I took deep breaths through my nose and thought that no matter how life should turn out and however far I travelled I would always remember this place as it was just now, and miss it. When I turned round I could see across the valley through a lattice of fir and pine, I saw the river winding and glittering below, I saw the red-tiled roof of Barkald's sawmill further south by the river bank and several small farmsteads on the green patches beside the narrow band of water. I knew the families who lived in them and knew how many people there were in each house, and if I did not see our cottage on the far bank I could point out exactly behind which trees it lay, and I wondered if my father was still asleep, or if he was walking around looking for me and without worrying wondering where I had gone, whether I would come home soon, whether perhaps he should start making breakfast, and I could suddenly feel how hungry I was.

'Here it is,' Jon said. 'There.' He pointed out a big spruce a little way from the path. We stood still.

'It's a big one,' I said.

'It's not *that*,' Jon said. 'Come.' He walked over to the tree and started to climb. It was not difficult, the lowest branches were strong and long, hung heavily down and were easy to get hold of, and in no time he was several

metres up, and I followed. He climbed quickly, but after
about ten metres he stopped and sat there waiting until we
were at the same height, and there was plenty of room,
we could sit side by side each on our thick branch. He
pointed to a place further out on the branch he sat on,
where it divided into two. A bird's nest hung down from
the fork, it was like a deep bowl or almost an ice-cream
cone. I had seen many nests but never such a tiny one, so
light, so perfectly formed of moss and feathers. And it did
not hang. It hovered.

'It's the goldcrest,' said Jon in a low voice. 'Second
brood.' He bent forward, stretched out his hand towards
the nest and put three fingers down in the feather-covered
opening, then brought up an egg that was so little I could
only sit there staring. He balanced the egg in his fingertips
and held it towards me so I could look at it closely, and it
made me dizzy to see and to think that in just a few weeks
this tiny oval would be transformed into a living bird
with wings that could take off from the high branches
and dive down and yet never hit the ground but with
will and instinct shoot upwards and nullify the force of
gravity. And I said it aloud:

'Christ,' I said. 'It's weird that something so little can
come alive and just fly away,' and maybe it was not that
well put and certainly far less than the rushing, airy feeling I felt inside me. But something happened at that moment that I had no way of understanding, for when I
raised my eyes and looked up at Jon's face it was strained
and totally white. Whether it was the few words I had uttered, or the egg he was holding, I shall never know, but
something made him change so suddenly, and he looked
me straight in the eye as if he had never seen me before,
and for once he did not squint, and his pupils were big

and black. And then he opened his hand and dropped
the egg. It fell along the trunk, and I followed it with my
eyes and saw it hit one of the branches further down and
break and dissolve into little pale fragments that swirled
around on all sides, and they fell like snowflakes, almost
weightless, and gently drifted away. Or that is the way I
remember it, and I could not recall anything ever making me so desperate. I looked up at Jon again, and he had
already bent forward, and with one hand he tore the nest
free of the split in the branches, held it out at arm's length
and crushed it to powder between his fingers only a few
centimetres from my eyes. I wanted to say something but
could not utter a word. Jon's face was a chalk-white mask
with an open mouth, and from that mouth came sounds
that made my blood run cold, I had never heard anything
like it; throaty noises like an animal I had never seen
and had no wish to see. He opened his hand again and
slammed his palm against the tree trunk and rubbed it on
the bark, and small flakes fluttered down, and finally all
that was left was a smear I couldn't look at. I closed my
eyes and kept them shut, and when I opened them again
Jon was a good way down. He almost slid from branch to
branch, I looked straight down at his unruly brown hair,
and he did not once look up. For the last few metres he
just let himself drop, and he landed on firm ground with
a thud I heard right up where I was sitting, and then he
fell on his knees like an empty sack and beat his forehead
on the ground, and stayed there huddled up for what
seemed an eternity, and for the whole of that eternity I
held my breath without stirring. I didn't understand what
had happened, but I felt it was my fault. I just didn't
know why. At last he stood up stiffly and started to walk

down the path. I let my breath out and drew it slowly in again, there was a whistle in my chest, I heard it clearly, it sounded like asthma. I knew a man who had asthma, he lived just up our street in Oslo. It sounded like that when he breathed. I've got asthma, I thought, shit, that's how you get asthma. When something happens. And then I started to climb down, not as fast as Jon, more as if each branch was a landmark I had to hold on to a long time so as not to miss one single thing that was important, and the whole time I *thought* about breathing.

Was it then the weather changed? I think it was. I stood on the path, Jon was nowhere to be seen, vanished down the way we had come, and suddenly I heard a rushing sound above me in the trees. I looked up and saw the tops of the spruces sway and whip against each other, I saw tall pines bend in the wind, and I felt the forest floor sway beneath my feet. It was like standing on water, it made me dizzy, and I looked around me for something to hold on to, but everything was moving. The sky, which just now had been so transparently blue, was steely grey with a sickly yellow light over the ridge on the other side of the valley. And then there was a violent flash over the ridge. It was followed by a crash I could feel all over my body, I sensed the temperature dropping, and my arm began to hurt where the barbed wire had cut it. I started walking as fast as I could, almost running, down the path we had come up, towards the horse paddock. When I was there I looked over the fence and in through the trees, but there were no horses that I could see there now, and for a moment I thought of taking the short cut across the clearing, but then instead I went along the fence on the outside, for the full circuit until I met the path to the road. I turned left there and started to run down, and the wind had stopped, the forest was breathlessly still, and the newly discovered asthma had my chest in a fierce grip.

Then I was standing on the road. The first drops hit my forehead. I caught sight of Jon further down. He had not been running, he was too close for that, and he was not walking fast, he was not walking slowly either. He just walked. I thought maybe I should call to him and ask him to wait, but I was not sure I had the breath in me. Besides, there was something about his figure that made me hold back, so I started to walk after him and kept the same distance between us the whole way, up past Barkald's farm where now the windows were brightly lit against the dark sky above, and I wondered if he was standing inside watching us and knowing where we had been. I looked up in the air hoping that the few drops I had felt would be just that, but then there was another flash above the hills and a crash at the same moment. I had never been afraid of thunder, and I wasn't afraid now, but I knew that when lightning and thunder came so close together it could strike anywhere close to me. It was a special feeling to walk along the road without any shelter at all. And then the rain came at me like a wall, and suddenly I was behind that wall and wet right through in a few seconds, and if I had been naked it would not have made any difference. The whole world was grey with water, and I could hardly glimpse Jon walking a hundred metres ahead of me. But I didn't need him to show me the way, I knew where I had to go. I turned off onto the path through Barkald's meadow, and if I hadn't already been wet, the tall grass would have made my trousers sticky and heavy. But that didn't matter now. I thought, now

Barkald will have to wait for several days before mowing the grass, to let it dry. You can't cut wet grass. And I
wondered if he would ask my father and me to help with
the haymaking as he had the year before, and I wondered whether Jon had taken the boat and rowed across
the river alone or if he was waiting for me on the bank. I
could walk back up the road towards the shop and down
again on the other side through the forest, but that was a
long, hard way. Or I could swim across. The water would
be cold now, and the current strong. I was freezing in my
wet clothes; it would be better without them. I stopped on
the path and started to pull my sweater off and my shirt.
It wasn't easy, they stuck to my body, but eventually I
managed to get them off and I rolled them into a bundle
under my arm. Everything was so wet it was almost ridiculous, and the rain beat down on my bare torso and
warmed me up in some strange way. I ran my hand over
my skin, and felt hardly anything at all, both skin and
fingers were numb, and I was tired and sleepy. How good
it would be, I thought, to lie down just for a bit and close
my eyes. I walked on a few steps. I wiped the water from
my face with my hand. I felt dizzy. And then I was right
beside the river, and I had not heard it. Jon sat in front
of me in the boat. His hair, which usually stood on end
in stiff tufts, was wet through and plastered to his skull.
He looked at me through the rain as he backed the oars to
keep the stern of the boat towards the bank, but he did
not say anything.

'Hi,' I said, and walked clumsily down the last few
metres over the smooth round stones. I tripped once, but
didn't fall, and I got into the boat and sat down on the
rear thwart. He started to row as soon as I was aboard, and

it was hard, I could see that, we had the current against us and we moved slowly. He was going to row me all the way home even though he must have been tired. He lived downstream himself, and I wanted to say it was not necessary, he could just row me straight across, I could walk the last bit myself. But I did not say a word. I couldn't.

At last we were there. Jon turned the boat with a valiant effort and edged it close enough for me to step straight onto the bank. And I did, and stayed on shore looking at him.

'So long,' I said. 'See you tomorrow.' But he didn't reply. Just lifted the oars free of the water and let the boat drift as he stared back, his eyes with a narrow look I knew already then I would never forget.

3

Back to his youth.

WE HAD COME OUT TWO WEEKS EARLIER, my father and I, by train from Oslo, and then on the
bus from Elverum for hours and hours. That bus worked a
stopping routine I never understood, but it certainly did
stop often, and sometimes I slept on the hot seat in the
baking sun, and when I woke up again and looked out
the window, it seemed we had not gone a millimetre further, for what I saw was the same view I had seen *before*
I fell asleep; a winding gravel road with fields on both
sides and farms with white-painted homesteads and red-
painted barns, and some were small and some were larger,
and the cows behind barbed-wire fences next to the road
lay in the grass chewing the cud with half-closed eyes in
the sunshine, and almost all of them were brown and only
some had patches of white on brown or black, and then
the forest behind the farms with its shades of blue rising
to an unchanging ridge.

That trip took all day more or less, and the odd thing
is that I did not get bored. I liked looking out the window
until my eyelids grew heavy and hot, and I fell asleep and
woke up again and looked out the window for the thou-
sandth time or more, or I turned round and looked over
to where my father sat through the whole trip with his
nose in a book on something technical, something about
house building or machines, about motors, he was mad
about such things. Then he would raise his head and look

at me and nod and smile, and I smiled back, and then he
dived down again, back into his book. And I slept and
dreamt about warm things, soft things, and when I woke
up for the last time it was because my father was shaking
my shoulder.

'Hi, chief,' he said and I opened my eyes and looked
around. The bus had stopped, the engine was switched
off, we were in the shade of the big oak tree in front of
the shop. I saw the path to the bridge over the river and
the river was narrow just there and foaming as it dropped
down the rapids, and the low sun sparkled in the spray.
We were the last passengers to leave. This was the final
stop. The bus could go no further, from here we had to
walk, and I thought it was just like my father, to take me
as far as he possibly could where it still was called Norway,
and I asked no questions about why precisely *here,* for it
was as if he was testing me, and I did not mind that. I
trusted my father.

We took our bags and gear from the luggage compartment at the back of the bus and started to walk towards
the bridge. In the middle we stopped and gazed down at
the rushing, almost green water, and we held on to our
bamboo fishing rods, beat them against the newly carpen-
tered wooden rail and we spat in the river, and my father
said:

'Just you wait, Jacob!'

Jacob was his name for all the fish, whether in the sea-
salt Oslo fjord at home with his chest right over the rail
and his face in a scornful smile at the water, with a play-
fully boxing fist over the deep; just you wait, Jacob, now
we're coming to get you, or in the river here that came

flowing in a semicircle crossing the border from Sweden and down through this village and back into Sweden a few kilometres further south. And I remembered the year before when I had gazed down into the whirling water and wondered whether in some way or other it was possible to see or feel or taste that the water was really Swedish and was only on loan this side of the border. But I was so much younger then and didn't know much about the world, and after all it was just a fancy. We stood on the bridge, my father and I, and we looked at each other and smiled, and I for one felt the sense of expectation spreading through my stomach.

'How goes it?' he said.

'Fine,' I said, and could not help laughing.

Now I walked up the path from the river in the rain. Behind me Jon was in the boat sailing down on the current. I wondered if he was talking aloud to himself, as I often did when I was alone, describing what I had just done and pondering for and against and ending by saying I hadn't had any choice. But probably he didn't.

My whole body was freezing cold, my teeth chattering. I carried my sweater and shirt under my arm, but it was too late to put them on again. The sky was darker now than it usually was at night. My father had lit the paraffin lamp in the cabin, there was a warm and yellow light in the windows, and grey smoke whirled up from the chimney and was immediately beaten down onto the roof by the wind, and water and smoke ran down the slates in a blend that looked like a grey porridge. It was a weird sight.

The door was ajar. I went right over to the porch and sniffed the smell of fried bacon filtering out of the shining crack. I stopped under the little eave. For the first time in ages the rain stopped slamming down on my head. I stood there for a minute or two, then opened the door wide and went in. My father was at the wood stove making breakfast. I stood on the threshold dripping onto the rag rug. He hadn't heard me. I didn't know what the time was, but I was sure he had postponed the cooking as long as he could. Over his shirt he had on an old sweater that was full of holes, which he liked to wear when he was working. He had not shaved since we arrived. His beard was growing. Hairy and free, he would say, stroking his chin. This was a man I liked. I coughed, and he turned and looked at me with his head on one side. I waited for him to say something.

'Blow me, what a wet lad,' he said.

I nodded. 'Oh yes,' I said between chattering teeth.

'Stay right there.' He pulled the frying pan off the heat, went into the bedroom and came back with a big towel.

'Off with your shoes and trousers,' he said. I did as he told me. It wasn't easy. Then I stood there naked on the rug. I felt like a little boy again.

'Come to the stove.' I went to the stove. He put two new logs in and closed the small door. Through the damper I saw the flames leap up, and waves of heat welled out of the black cast iron, almost painful on my skin. Then he wound the towel round me and began to rub, carefully at first and then harder and harder. It felt as if I was bursting into flames, it was like the Red Indians rubbing two sticks together to make fire. I was a stiff, dry stick, then I became a red-hot mass.

'Look, hold on to it yourself,' he said. I held the towel firmly round my shoulders, and he went into the bedroom again and came out with clean trousers, a thick sweater and socks. I got dressed very slowly.

'Hungry?' he asked.

'Yes,' I said, and then I didn't say any more for a long time. I sat down at the table. He served bacon and egg and bread he had baked himself in the old oven, and he cut it into thick slices and spread it with margarine. I ate everything he set before me, and he too sat down to eat. We heard the rain battering the roof and it rained on the river and on Jon's boat and on the road to the shop and on Barkald's meadows, it rained over the forest and the horses in their paddock and all the birds' nests in all the trees, over moose and over hare, and on every roof in the village, but inside the cottage it was warm and dry. The stove was crackling, and I ate until my plate was completely clean, and my father ate with a half smile on his mouth as if it was just any old morning, but it was *not*, and then I suddenly felt tired and bent over, put my head on my hands on the table and there I fell asleep.

When I woke up I was lying under the duvet in the bottom bunk, which was really my father's place. I still had all my clothes on. The sun shone in through the window from the sky behind the cabin, and I realised it must be long after twelve. I pushed the duvet aside and swung myself out of bed and put my feet on the floor. I felt great. There was a tenderness down one side, but nothing to worry about. I went into the main room. The door was wide open and there was sun in the yard. The moist grass was glittering and a woolly carpet of steam hung a metre above the ground. A fly buzzed in the window. My father stood by the cupboard in one corner, taking groceries out of his backpack and putting them on the shelves. He had walked the long way to the shop and back while I slept.

He saw me at once, stopped what he was doing and stood there with a bag in one hand. It was very still, and he was very serious.

'How are you feeling?' he said.

'Fine,' I said. 'I feel just fine.'

'That's good,' he said, and then fell quiet, and then he said:

'When you were out this morning, were you with Jon, then?'

'Yes,' I said.

'What were you doing?'

'We were out stealing horses.'

'*What's* that you say?' My father was taken aback. 'Which horses then?'

'Barkald's horses. We weren't really stealing them. We were just going to ride them. But we call it stealing to make it more exciting.' I smiled cautiously, but he didn't smile back. 'I wasn't too successful,' I said, 'I was thrown off, right over the barbed-wire fence.' I held out my arm to show the cut, but he looked me straight in the face.

'How was Jon?'

'Jon? He was the same as usual. Except at the end. He wanted to show me the eggs in a goldcrest's nest high up in a spruce tree, and then suddenly he crushed the whole nest, like this,' I said and held my arm out again and made a squeezing gesture with my fist, and my father put the last bag into the cupboard, still looking at me and nodding, and then he closed the cupboard door and stroked his bearded chin, and I said:

'And then he went off, and then the thunderstorm started.'

My father took his backpack over to the door and put it down there, stood looking out at the yard with his back to me. He scratched his neck, then turned and came back and sat down at the table, and said:

'Do you want to know what they're all talking about at the shop?'

I didn't particularly want to know what people were talking about at the shop, but he would tell me anyway.

'Yes,' I said.

The previous day Jon had been out with his gun, hunting hares as usual. I didn't know why he was so mad about shooting hares, but it had come to be a speciality for him, and he was good, he got one out of two. And that was not bad considering what a small, swift creature the hare was. I didn't know whether his family ate all those hares. They might get a bit tired of that. Anyway, he came home with two of them dangling by an ear on a cord, and he smiled like the sun, for he had fired two shots that morning, and both had hit the mark. That was a rare triumph even for him. Now he was home looking round for his mother and father to show them his booty, but his mother was visiting friends in Innbygda, and his father was in the forest. In his hurry to go out he had forgotten that, he did not notice who was at home, but it was his job to look after the twins. He put his gun down in the hall and hung the cord with the hares on a peg and ran through the house to find his brothers, but they were nowhere to be seen, and then he ran out into the yard again and round the shed and round the barn, but he did not find them. Now he panicked. He ran down to the river and waded out beside the jetty they had there, turned and looked along the bank upriver, and he looked downriver, but all he saw was a squirrel in a spruce tree.

'Damn tree-bear,' he said. He bent down to the water and ran his hands through it as if to pull it aside so he could see better, but of course it was pointless, the water only came up to his knees and was perfectly clear. He straightened up and drew a deep breath and tried to think, and then he heard a shot from the house.

The gun. He had forgotten to make the gun safe, he had not removed the last cartridge, something he always did when he got home. That weapon was the only thing of value he owned, and he had looked after it and polished it and kept it in good order as if it was his baby, and he had done that ever since his father gave it to him for his twelfth birthday, with strict exhortations on what it should be used for, and in particular what it should *not* be used for. And he always put it at half cock and took out the cartridges and hung it in place in the closet on a hook high on the wall. But now he had just put it down in the hall because it suddenly came to his mind what he had forgotten, that he was the one responsible for the twins, who were at home alone. They were just ten years old.

Jon splashed out of the river and ran a stretch along the bank, then on in a straight line for the house, and it seemed such a long way, and his trouser legs were wet and heavy right up to the knee, and his shoes squelched and made a squishing sound with each step that he took and it made him feel sick. Halfway to the house he saw his father come running out of the forest on the other side of the farmhouse. He had never ever seen his father run, and the sight of the big heavy man leaping out from the trees and into the yard with long, pounding strides and his arms clumsily raised to shoulder height as if he was running through water was so terrifying that Jon stopped and sank down onto the grass. Whatever had happened it was too late now, and his father would be first into the house, and Jon knew he did not want to see what had happened.

What had happened was that the twins had been playing in the basement the whole morning with cast-off clothes and worn-out shoes. Then they came running upstairs laughing, and stumbling into the corridor through the basement door, and there they saw the hares hanging on the peg and the gun leaning against the wall. It was Jon's gun, that they knew, and their big brother Jon was their hero, and if they had the same role models as I did at that age, he was their Davy Crockett and Hartsfoot and Huckleberry Finn in one person. Everything Jon did could be mimicked and turned into a game.

Lars got there first, he grabbed the gun and swung it around and shouted:

'Look at me now!' And then he pulled the trigger. The report and the shock from the butt sent him to the floor with a shriek, and he did not aim at anything, he just wanted to hold the wonderful gun and be *Jon,* and he might have hit the woodbox, or the small window over the steps, or the photograph of grandfather with his long beard that hung just above the peg in a frame painted the colour of gold, or the light bulb that hung there without a shade and was never switched off so that anyone out in the dark would see its light in the window and never get lost. But he did not hit any of those things, he hit Odd straight in the heart at close range. And if this had been something that happened in a western, those porous pages would claim that the very name of Odd had been written on that cartridge, or it was written in the stars or on one of the pages in the fat book of Destiny. That nothing anyone could have done or said would have made the lines that met in *that* burning moment point any other way. That powers other than those controlled by man had made the mouth of that gun point in precisely that direction. But that was not how it was, and Jon knew it where he lay huddled up on the grass of the meadow and saw his father come out of the house with his brother in his arms, and the only book where the name of Odd was written and could not be crossed out was the church registry book.

My father could not have told me all this, not with all the details; but that is the way it is printed in my memory, and I do not know whether I began filling out this painting at once, or if it is something I have done over the years. But the cold facts of the matter could not be contested, what had happened had happened indeed, and my father looked enquiringly at me across the table as if *I* could say something sensible about all this, because I maybe knew the people in the drama better than he did, but all I saw was Jon's white face and the rain falling on the rushing water of the river as he pushed off and let the boat drift out and down with the current towards the house where he lived and those who waited for him there.

'Still, that's not the worst of it,' said my father.

Early in the morning, the day before Lars shot his twin brother Odd, their mother had been given a lift to Innbygda in the van that delivered goods to the shop. The following day, the day it all happened, their father was going to fetch her with horse and cart. Their horse was called Bramina, she was a fifteen-year-old bay, a sturdy Norwegian horse with a white blaze and white socks. She was nice looking, I thought, but, not light on her feet exactly, and Jon thought she had a touch of hay fever, which caused her to breathe heavily, and that was pretty unusual for a horse. The trip with her to Innbygda and back took most of the day.

The father stood out in the yard with the dead boy in his arms. His eldest son lay on the grass completely still as if he too was dead. He knew he had to go. He had said he would. He had no choice. And if he was to get there in time he had to leave at once. He turned and went into the house again. Lars stood in the hall, stiff and silent, and his father saw him, but he could not think about more than one big thing at a time, and he went into the bedroom and laid Odd on the marriage bed, found a blanket and covered the small body. He changed his blood-soaked shirt and he changed his trousers and went to harness Bramina. Out of the corner of his eye he saw that Jon was on his feet and walking slowly towards the stable. By the time the horse was between the shafts Jon was there. His father turned round and seized him by the shoulders—much too roughly, he thought later—but the boy said not a word.

'You'll have to look after Lars while I'm gone. That at least you can manage,' and he looked across at the steps where Lars had come out into the sun and stood blinking in the strong light. Their father ran a hand over his face, closed his eyes for a moment, then he cleared his throat and climbed onto the box, whipped up the horse and the cart began to move and turned out through the gate and down to the main road, up past the shop and then slowly the long way to Innbygda.

Jon took Lars out in the boat with him and down the river to fish, he could not think of anything else, and they were away for hours. What they talked about I have never been able to imagine. Maybe they did not speak at all. Maybe they just stood on the bank, each with his rod, fishing; casting and reeling in again, casting and reeling in, with a good distance between them, and nothing around them but the forest and a great silence. That I can imagine.

When they returned they went in the barn with their small catch and sat there waiting. Not once did they go into the house. Late in the evening they heard the sound of Bramina's hooves on the gravel and the cart rolling up the road. They looked at each other. They would really have liked to sit on there for a while longer. Then Jon got to his feet, and so did Lars, and they held hands for the first time since the twins were quite little, and went into the yard and watched the cart come towards them up the drive and stop, and they heard Bramina's asthmatic breathing and their father's comforting words to the horse; kind words, gentle words, words they had never heard him say to a human being.

Their mother sat on the box in the blue dress with the yellow flowers on it, her handbag in her lap, and she smiled at them and said:

'Here I am, home again, that's nice, isn't it?' and she rose, put her foot on the wheel and jumped down.

'Where is Odd?' she said.

Jon looked up at his father, but he did not look back, he just stared at the barn wall and chewed as if his mouth was full of tobacco. He had not told her. The whole long way through the forest, just the two of them, and he had not told her anything.

The funeral took place three days later. My father asked if we should go and I said yes. It was my first funeral. One of my mother's brothers had been shot by the Germans when he tried to escape from a police station somewhere in Sørlandet on the south coast in 1943, but of course I was not there when it happened, and I don't even know if there was a funeral.

I remember two things about Odd's funeral. One of them is that my father and Jon's father not once looked each other in the eye. My father did shake his hand and say:

'Condolences,' a word that sounded completely foreign, and he was the only one who used it that day, but they did not *look* at each other.

The other thing was Lars. When we went out of the church and stood by the open grave he grew more and more restless, and when the priest was halfway through the ceremony and the little coffin was to be lowered down with a rope round each handle, he could not bear it any longer and tore himself free from his mother and ran away among the headstones until he was almost out of the churchyard, and started to run in a circle right over by the stone wall. He ran round and round with his head lowered and his eyes on the ground, and the longer he ran the slower the priest spoke, and at first there were just a few people in the black-clad flock who turned round, but gradually more did, until at last they had all turned to look at Lars instead of the coffin that held his brother, and it went on until a neighbour walked quietly across the grass, stopped at the edge of the circle, caught Lars as he ran by and picked him up. His legs were still running, but he did not utter a sound. I looked over at Jon and he looked back at me, and I shook my head slightly, but he made no sign in return, just stared straight into my eyes without blinking. And I remember thinking that we would never go out stealing horses together again, and it made me sadder than anything that happened at the churchyard. That is what I remember. Which makes it three things in all.

4

Back to his Youth

THERE WERE TREES ON THE LAND my father had
bought as well as pasture. Mostly spruce, but pine as
well, and here and there a slim birch was almost squeezed
in between the darker trunks, and all of them grew right
down from the river bank, where in some mysterious
way a wooden cross had been nailed up on a pine tree
that grew at the edge of the pebbles, almost overhanging
the rushing water. Then the forest continued almost full
circle around the yard and the cottage with the shed and
the meadow behind it and on to the narrow road where
our land ended. That road was really hardly more than a
sparsely gravelled track through the rows of spruce with
roots crisscrossing it, and ran parallel to the river some
way away on the east side right up to the wooden bridge
where it turned towards the 'centre' with the shop and
the church. That was the route we took when we arrived
on the bus at the end of June, or when some idiot had
left our boat on the wrong side; east or west according
to where we happened to be. As a rule the idiot was me.
Otherwise we walked over Barkald's field alongside the
fence and rowed across the river.

Around noon our cottage was shaded from the sun for
a couple of hours by the dense forest to the south, and
I wondered whether that was the reason for my father's
decision to chop the whole creek of shit down and sell
it as timber. I am certain he needed the money, but I had
not realised it was so urgent; and that we had travelled

up to this river at all, and for the second time in a row at that, it was my thought that he was in need of the time and the peace to plan out a different life from the one that was behind him and that he had to do this in a different place with a different view from the one we had where we lived in Oslo. We're at a crossroads now, he had said. I alone was allowed to go with him, and that gave me a status my sister could not boast, because she had to stay on in town with my mother, although she was three years older than I was.

'I don't want to go anyway, I would just have to wash up while you two were out fishing. I'm not stupid,' she said, and she was probably right there, and I thought I understood what my father meant, and I heard him say more than once that he could not think with women around. I never had that problem myself. On the contrary.

Later on I have thought that maybe he did not mean *all* women.

But it was the shade he talked about; that bloody shade, he said, after all, it is holiday time, damn it, and he cursed as he sometimes would when my mother was not present. She grew up in a town where she claimed they swore the whole time, and now she did not want to hear any more of that. Personally I thought it was fine to be free of the sunshine for some time during the hot hours when the forest held its breath in the strong light and produced scents that made me sluggish and drowsy and could make me fall asleep in the middle of the day.

Whatever the reason, he had made his decision. Most of the trees were to be felled and the trunks hauled to the river and floated down on the current to a sawmill in

Sweden. I wondered at that because Barkald had a saw only a kilometre downstream, but it was just a farm saw and was maybe too small and not able to cope with the quantity we would be sending. The Swedes though were not willing to buy the timber at the spot, as the custom was, but would only pay for what arrived at the timber yard. Nor would they take responsibility for the rafting. Not in July, they said.

'Maybe we should just take a little at a time,' I suggested. 'A little now and a little next year?'

'I am the one who decides when my timber is to be felled,' he said. That was not what I meant, whether it was his decision or not, but I left it there. It was not important to me. My concern was whether he would let me join in the drift, and who else would be there, for it was heavy work, and certainly dangerous if you did not know what you were doing, and as far as I knew my father had never done any logging before. And he probably hadn't, I can see that today, but he had so much self-confidence he could take on almost anything and believe he would succeed.

But first it was time for haymaking. It did not rain much after the thunderstorm, and the grass dried out in a couple of days, and one morning Barkald came over to us with his hair newly brushed and his hands in his pockets to ask if we might consider putting in a few days with the hayfork. He was sure that last year's hay would have gone down the drain had it not been for the muscle my father and I had put into it, mine in particular, I was to understand from his flattering words, but I was old enough to realise that what he was really after was free labour. But he was right, of course. We had worked hard.

My father stroked his bearded chin, squinted at the sun for a moment before he glanced sideways down at me where we stood on the steps.

'What say you, Trond T.?' he asked. Tobias is my middle name, but I would never use it, and the T. only turned up when my father wanted to sound a tad serious and it was a signal to me that now there was room to fool around a bit.

'Ye-e-es,' I said. 'There might just be a possibility there.'

'We do have some work of our own to see to as well,' he said.

'That's true,' I said. 'We have a few things to get out of the way, it's not that, but maybe we could squeeze in a day or two, we might just about manage.'

'We might, but it won't be easy,' said my father.

'Yeah, it will be hard,' I said. 'One would have to say that a barter in kind would probably come in handy.'

'You're right there,' said my father, looking at me with curiosity. 'Bartering surely couldn't be a bad thing.'

'A horse, with harness,' I said. 'For a few days of next week or the one after.'

'Just so,' my father said with a broad smile. 'Right to a tee. What do you say to that, Barkald?'

Barkald had been standing there in the yard with a be-wildered expression on his face as he listened to our con-torted dialogue, and now he stepped right into the trap. He ran his hands through his hair and said:

'Yes, well, I don't see why not. You are welcome to have Brona,' he said, and I could see he wanted to ask what we actually needed the horse for, but he felt he had somehow lost his track and the last thing he wanted was to make a fool of himself.

Barkald said he would start mowing the following day when what little dew there was had dried off, we should just turn up in the north meadow, and then he raised his hand in farewell, obviously glad to be off, and made his way down to the river to board his boat, and my father put his hands to his sides and looked at me and said:

'That was brilliant, how did you come to think of that?' He had no idea how carefully I had been over the logging operation in my mind, and as I had not heard him mention anything about a horse, I put my oar in, for I knew we could not drag the tree trunks to the river with our bare hands. But I did not reply, just shrugged with a smile. He grabbed a tuft of my hair and shook my head gently.

'You're no dimwit,' he said, and he was right. I had always thought so: that I was no fool.

Four days had passed since Odd's funeral, and I had not seen Jon since then. It felt strange. I woke up in the morning listening for his footsteps in the yard and on the steps, and I listened for the creak of oars in their rowlocks and the slight bump when his boat hit the stones on the shore. But each morning all was quiet, apart from the birds singing and the wind in the treetops and the sounds of bells when the cattle from the summer dwellings north and south of us were driven up into the hills behind the cabin to graze all day on the green hillside until the milkmaids came out on the meadows and walked up to the road to sing them home at five o'clock. I lay in my bunk by the open window and heard the crisp metallic clanging of the bells change with the changing terrain thinking I would not wish to be anywhere else than in this cottage with my father, no matter what had happened, and every time I dressed and Jon was not there at the door, I sensed a flash of relief. Then I felt ashamed, and there was a soreness in my throat, and it could take several hours before that soreness disappeared.

And I did not see him by the river, did not see him with his fishing rod along the bank or in the boat on his way up or down, and my father did not ask me whether we had been out together, and I did not ask my father whether he had seen him. That's the way it was. We just had breakfast, put our working clothes on and went down to the old rowboat that had been included in the purchase of the cottage, and rowed across the water.

The sun was shining. I sat on the stern thwart with my eyes closed against the light and my father's familiar face as he rowed with easy strokes, and I thought about how it must feel to lose your life so early. Lose your life, as if you held an egg in your hand, and then dropped it, and it fell to the ground and broke, and I knew it could not feel like anything at all. If you were dead, you were dead, but in the fraction of a second just before; whether you realised then it was the end, and what that felt like. There was a narrow opening there, like a door barely ajar, that I pushed towards, because I *wanted* to get in, and there was a golden light in that crack that came from the sunlight on my eyelids, and then suddenly I slipped inside, and I was certainly there for a little flash, and it did not frighten me at all, just made me sad and astonished at how quiet everything was. When I opened my eyes, the feeling stayed with me. I looked across the water towards the far bank, and it was still there. I looked at my father's face as if from a place far off, and I blinked several times

and drew a deep breath, and perhaps I trembled a little,
for he smiled enquiringly and said:

'How goes it with you, chief?'

'I am alright,' I said, after a pause. But when we came
alongside the bank and tied the boat up and walked
along the fence over the meadow, I felt it somewhere inside
me; a small remnant, a bright yellow speck that perhaps
would never leave me.

When we came up to the north meadow there were already people there. Barkald himself stood by the mowing machine with the reins in his hand, ready to get on.
I recognised the horse, my crotch still felt sore after our
ride together, and there were two men from the village
and a woman I had not seen before, who did not look like
a farmer's wife but might be a relative of the people living here, and Mrs Barkald stood talking to Jon's mother.
The two had put their hair up in loose topknots and wore
faded dresses of flowered cotton, which clung to their
bodies, and bare legs in calf-length boots, and they held
rakes with handles twice as long as they were tall. We
heard their voices all the way down on the track through
the morning air, and Jon's mother was different out here
in the meadow than at home in their cramped house, and
it was so palpable I saw it at once, and my father obviously
noticed the same thing. Almost unwillingly we turned
our heads and exchanged glances and recognised in each
other's eyes what the other had seen. My face grew hot
and I felt tense and at the same time ill at ease, but I did
not know if it was due to my own surprising thoughts or
because I saw my father had thought as I did. When he
saw me blushing he laughed, softly, but not patronising

at all, I'll give him that. He just laughed. Almost with enthusiasm.

We walked up through the grass to the mower and
greeted Barkald and his wife, and Jon's mother shook
hands with us and thanked us for joining them at Odd's
funeral. She was solemn and slightly swollen around the
eyes, but not defeated. She was tanned in a nice way, her
dress blue, and her eyes were blue and glittering, and
she was only a few years younger than my own mother.
She was simply shining, and it was as if I saw her for the
first time in a clear light and I wondered whether it was
because of what had happened, whether something like
that could make a person stand out and be luminous. I
had to stare at the ground and across the meadow to avoid
her eyes, and then I went over to the pile of stakes where
the tools were and picked a hayfork to lean against while
I looked at nothing and waited for Barkald to get started.
My father stood talking for a while, then he came up too,
picked a hayfork from the grass between two rolls of steel
wire, drove it into the ground and waited as I did while
we avoided looking at each other, and Barkald, who sat
on the mowing machine seat, urged on the horse, lowered
the cutters and began to move.

The field had been divided into four sections, into each
of which would go a rack, and Barkald cut the grass in a
straight line along the middle of the first section. A few
metres from the edge of the meadow we knocked a strong
peg into the ground at an angle with a sledgehammer,
secured the end of one roll of wire around the peg and fastened it firmly, and then it was my job to lift the reel by the
two handles shiny with wear and unroll the wire while I
held it taut and walked backwards in the section Barkald

had cut. It was heavy, after a few metres my wrists began to ache, and my shoulders hurt because I had to do three things at once with the heavy reel, and my muscles were not warm yet. As the wire gradually unrolled it became easier, but by then I was that much more exhausted, and there was suddenly an opposition to everything that was physical and I grew mad and did not want anyone there to see I was such a city boy, particularly while Jon's mother was looking at me with that blinding blue gaze of hers, I'd make up my own mind when it should hurt, and if it should show or not, and I pushed the pain down into my body so my face would not give me away, and with arms raised I unrolled the reel and the wire ran out until I came to the end of the meadow, and there I put the reel down in the short stubble of newly mown grass, the wire taut, all as calmly as I could and just as calmly straightened up and pushed my hands into my pockets and let my shoulders sink down. It felt as if knives were cutting my neck and I walked very slowly over to the others. When I passed my father, he raised his hand casually and stroked my back and said quietly:

'You did good.' And that was enough. The pain vanished and I was already eager for the next thing.

Barkald had finished mowing the first part of the field and had cut the first swathe of the next, and now he stood by the horse waiting for us to do the rest. He was the boss, and according to my father he was one of those who worked best sitting down and rested standing up, that is if it didn't go on too long, for then he had to sit down again anyway. If there was anything he needed a rest from. I wasn't so sure about that. Driving that horse wasn't exactly exhausting. It had done the job so many times before it could do it with its eyes shut, and was bored now and wanted to move on, but was not allowed to, for Barkald was systematic and had no plan to mow the whole field in one go. It was one section first and then the next, while the sun was shining from a cloudless sky and promised more of the same. The day was so far advanced now that we could feel the backs of our shirts getting soaked with sweat, and each time we lifted a heavy load it ran from our foreheads. The sun was right in the south and there was hardly a shadow in the valley, the river, sparkling, wound its way along, and we could hear it rushing down the rapids under the bridge by the shop. I picked up an armful of poles and carried them out, distributing them at suitable intervals along the steel wire and went back empty-handed for more, and my father and one of the men from the village measured out lengths and with a crowbar made holes every two metres along the line, alternately on each side of the wire and thirty-two in all, and my father was down to his singlet now, white against his dark hair and his tanned skin and his smooth shining upper arms, and the big fencing crowbar went up and then heavily down with a sucking sound in the damp earth, like a machine, my father, and happily, my father, and Jon's mother in tow planting the stakes in the holes the whole way along to the point where the steel wire reel was and a new peg was going down to keep the rack standing, and I could not stop watching them.

She stopped once and put the stake down and took a few steps to stand with her back turned and look down at the river with shaking shoulders. Then my father straightened his back and waited, gloved hands round the crowbar, and then she turned with her face alight and tear-stained, and my father smiled and nodded to her, his hair falling over his brow, and he lifted the crowbar again, and she smiled soberly back, came over and picked one stake up, and with a twisting movement she wedged it into the hole so that it stuck. And then they went on, in the same rhythm as before.

Neither Jon nor his father had come, although I had been certain they would, because they had been there the year before, but maybe they had other things to do, things of their own, or they just could not bring themselves to come. That *she* could was strange, in fact, but when I had watched her working for a while, I thought no more about it. Maybe my father would invite all three of them to the logging. That was not impossible, because Jon's father did have much experience of it, but on the other hand how would things go, if they went on as they had up to now, and could not look at each other?

When all the stakes were standing in a jagged row across the field, the steel wire had to be stretched at thigh height between them with a loop alternately to the right and the left so the wire would lie straight in the middle. The two men from the village took care of that job; one was tall and the other was short, and that was plainly a good combination, because they had done it before and were brisk and efficient at getting the wire to stretch taut as a guitar string right down to the last stake and lashed securely around the peg that Barkald had knocked in at the other end. We others picked our rakes up and walked out fanwise with the right distance between us and started to rake the grass from all sides towards the rack, and it was obvious at once why the handles were so long. They provided radius enough for us to cover the whole space together, and not so much as a straw was left behind, but it was tough on our palms with the rake rubbing forwards and backwards a thousand times, and we had to wear gloves to save the skin from being torn and prevent burns and blisters after one hour only. And then we filled the first wire, some with hayforks and balance and great precision, others with their hands, like my father and I, who did not have the same experience. But that went well too, and the inner side of our bare arms turned slowly green, and the wire filled up, and we fixed up another one and filled that one too, and then another, until we had five wires crammed full one above the other, and the top one with a slightly shallower layer of grass hung down like a thatched roof on each side, so when the rain came it would just run off, and the rack could stand there for months and the hay would be just as good right under the outermost layer. Barkald said it was almost as good as having it dry in the barn, that is if everything was done properly, and as far as I could see nothing was wrong. The rack stood as if it had been there forever across the landscape and lit by the sun with its long shadow behind it, and in harmony with every fold of the field and finally turned into a mere form, a primordial form, even if that was not the word I used then, and it gave me huge pleasure just to look at it. I can still feel the same thing today when I see a hayrack in a photograph from a book, but all that is a thing of the past now. No-one makes hay this way any more in this part of the country; today there is one man alone on a tractor, and then the drying on the ground and the mechanical turner and wrapping machines and huge plastic white cubes of stinking silage. So the feeling of pleasure slips into the feeling that time has passed, that it is very long ago, and the sudden feeling of being old.

5
Now

I DID NOT RECOGNISE HIM the first few times I saw him, so I just nodded when I passed by with Lyra, for my mind was not running on those lines, why should it be? When he was outside his cabin stacking piles of firewood under the eaves and I was on my way along the road thinking of other things entirely. Not even when he told me his name did it register. But after going to bed last night I began to wonder. There had been something about that man and the face I had seen in the wavering light of our torches. Now suddenly I am sure. Lars is Lars even though I saw him last when he was ten years old, and now he's past sixty, and if this had been something in a novel it would just have been irritating. I have in fact done a lot of reading particularly during the last few years, but earlier too, by all means, and I have thought about what I've read, and that kind of coincidence seems far-fetched in fiction, in modern novels anyway, and I find it hard to accept. It may be all very well in Dickens, but when you read Dickens you're reading a long ballad from a vanished world, where everything has to come together in the end like an equation, where the balance of what was once disturbed must be restored so that the gods can smile again. A consolation, maybe, or a protest against a world gone off the rails, but it is not like that any more, my world is not like that, and I have never gone along with those who believe our lives are governed by fate. They whine, they wash their hands and crave pity. I believe we shape our lives ourselves, at any rate I have shaped mine, for what it's worth, and I take complete responsibility. But of all the places I might have moved to, I had to land up precisely here.

Not that it changes anything. It doesn't change my plan for this place, doesn't change how it feels living here, all that is as before and I'm sure he did not recognise *me,* and that's the way I would like it to continue. But of course it does make *some* difference.

My plan for this place is quite simple. It is to be my final home. How long that might be for is something I haven't given much thought to. It is one day at a time here. And what I have to work out first is how I shall get through the winter, if there is a lot of snow. The road down to Lars' cabin is two hundred metres long, and there's another fifty on to the main road. With this back of mine it will not be possible to clear that stretch with a shovel. I could not have done it with my back as strong as it ever was. There wouldn't have been time for anything else.

Snow clearing is important, and a good battery in the car if it gets really cold. It is six kilometres to the district Co-op. And enough wood for the stove is important. There are two panel heaters in the house, but they are old and probably eat up more electricity than they give out heat. I could have bought a couple of modern oil-filled radiators on wheels, the type you can plug straight into the power point and pull around as required, but my idea is that the heat I cannot produce myself, I will have to do without. Luckily there was a large pile of old birchwood in the outhouse when I came here, but that is not nearly enough, and it's so dry that it will burn up fast, so a few days ago I cut down a dead spruce with the chainsaw I bought, and my current project is to cut up the spruce and split it into usable logs and stack them all on top of the old wood before it is too late. I have already dug deep into that birchwood pile.

The chainsaw is a Jonsered. Not that I think Jonsered is the best brand, but they only use Jonsereds round here, and the man I bought it from at the machine workshop in the village said they wouldn't touch any other make if I brought him a broken chain and wanted it repaired. It's not a new saw, but it has been overhauled recently and has a brand new chain, and the man seemed quite determined. So Jonsered rules here. And Volvo. I have never seen so many Volvos in one place; from the latest luxury models to old Amazons, more of the latter than the former, and I saw an old PV model too, in front of the post office, in 1999. That ought to tell me something about this place, but I'm not sure what, except that we are quite close to Sweden, and to inexpensive spare parts. Maybe it's as simple as that.

I get into the car and drive off. Down the road and across the river, past Lars' cottage and out onto the main road through the forest, and I see the lake sparkling through the trees on the right until suddenly it is behind me, and then it's across an open plain of yellow, long-since harvested fields on both sides. There are large flocks of crows flying over the fields. They make no sound in the sunlight. At the other end of the plain a sawmill lies beside a river, wider than the one I can see from my house but flowing into the same lake. Formerly it was used for rafting, which is why the sawmill is situated where it is, but that is long ago, and the sawmill could have been anywhere, because

timber is all transported by road nowadays, and it's no
joke to meet one of the heavily laden trucks with trailers
on a bend in a narrow country road. They drive like the
Greeks do and use the horn instead of braking. Only a few
weeks ago I had to drive into the ditch, the colossal brute
thundered past me well into my lane, and I just wrenched
the wheel over, and maybe I closed my eyes for a second
for I thought my hour had come, but only the glass of my
right indicator was smashed on a tree-stump. I sat there a
long time, though, with my forehead against the wheel. It
was almost dark, the engine had stopped, but my lights
were on, and when I lifted my head from the wheel, I saw
the lynx brightly outlined only fifteen metres in front of
the car. I had never seen a lynx before, but I knew what it
was that I was looking at. The evening was perfectly still
around us, and the lynx turned neither to right nor left. It
just walked. Softly, not wasting energy, filled with itself.
I can't recall when I last felt so alive as when I got the car
onto the road again and drove on. Everything that was me
lay taut and quivering just beneath my skin.

Next day at the shop I told them about the lynx. It was
most likely a dog, they said. No-one believed me. No-one
I saw that day had ever seen the lynx, so why should I,
who had lived there barely a month, be blessed with such
a thing? If I had been one of them I might have thought
the same, but I saw what I saw, I have the image of the big
cat somewhere inside me and can call upon it whenever I
like, and I hope that one day, or just as good, one night, I
shall see it again. That would be great.

I park in front of the Stat Oil station. The broken indicator. I still have not replaced the glass, or changed the
bulb for that matter, but have managed without it. It is

starting to get a bit too dark in the evenings to do without, besides it's illegal to drive without one. So I go in and talk to the man in the workshop. He glances out the window in the sliding door and says he will change the bulb at once and order the new glass from a car scrapyard.

'No sense in spending money on something new for an old car,' he says. And that's true, no doubt. The car is a ten-year-old Nissan station wagon, and I could easily have bought a new car, I can afford that, but in addition to the house purchase it would have eaten into my resources quite a lot, so I opted against it. In fact I had plans for a car with four-wheel drive, it would have been useful out here, but then I decided that a four-wheeler was a bit like cheating and a bit new-rich, and I ended up with this one, which has rear-wheel drive like everything else I've driven. I have already been to the mechanic with various problems, a worn-out dynamo among other things, and he says the same thing each time and orders from the same scrap dealer. It costs a fraction of new parts, and I also think he charges too little. But he whistles as he works and has his radio in the workshop tuned to the news channel, and the price policy is obviously deliberate. He is so friendly and obliging it bewilders me. I had actually expected some resistance, especially as I don't drive a Volvo. Maybe he's an outsider too.

I leave the car at the petrol station and walk past the church and over the crossroads to the shop. That is unusual. I've noticed that everyone here gets into the car and drives regardless of where they are going or how far it is. The Co-op is a hundred metres away, but I am the only one who *walks* outwith the parking place. I feel exposed and am happy to get into the shop.

I exchange greetings to right and left, they are used to me now and realise I am here to stay and that I am not one of the holiday cottage crew who pile out here in their mammoth cars every Easter and summer to fish by day and play poker and swig sundowners in the evening. It took some time before they started to ask questions, cautiously, in the queue for the check-out, and now everyone knows who I am and where I live. They know about my working life, how old I am, that my wife died three years ago in an accident I only just survived myself, that she was not my first wife, and that I have two grown-up children from an earlier marriage, and that they have children themselves. I have told them all that, including how when my wife died I did not want to go on working, and I pensioned myself off and started to look for a completely new place to live, and when I found the house I live in now I was really happy. They like hearing that, although everyone says I could have asked anybody round here and they would have told me what a state the house was in, that many people had wanted the place on account of its lovely situation but none of them felt like taking it on because of the work that was needed to make it fit to live in. Then I say it was just as well I didn't know, for then I would not have bought it, and not found out it is quite possible to live in if you do not demand too much at once, but just take one step at a time. That suits me fine, I say, I have plenty of time, I'm not going anywhere.

People like it when you tell them things, in suitable portions, in a modest, intimate tone, and they think they know you, but they do not, they know *about* you, for what they are let in on are facts, not feelings, not what your opinion is about anything at all, not how what has happened to you and how all the decisions you have made have turned you into who you are. What they do is they fill in with their own feelings and opinions and assumptions, and they compose a new life which has precious little to do with yours, and that lets you off the hook. No-one can touch you unless you yourself want them to. You only have to be polite and smile and keep paranoid thoughts at bay, because they will talk about you no matter how much you squirm, it is inevitable, and you would do the same thing yourself.

There is not much I want, just a loaf of bread and something to put on it, and that's soon done. I'm surprised at how unfilled my shopping baskets have become, how few things I need now I am alone. I suffer a sudden onset of meaningless melancholy and feel the eyes of the check-out lady on my forehead as I search for the money to pay, *the widower* is what she sees, they do not understand anything, and it is just as well.

'Here you are,' she says quietly in a voice soft as silk, as she gives me my change, and I say:

'Many thanks,' and I am on the verge of tears, for Christ's sake, and go out quickly with my purchases in a bag and across to the filling station. I have been lucky. They do not understand a thing.

He has changed the bulb for the indicator light. I put my bag on the passenger seat and walk between the pumps and into the shop. His wife is smiling behind the counter.

'Hi,' she says.

'Hi,' I say. 'That bulb. How much is it?'

'Not much. It can wait. How about a cup of coffee? Olav is taking five minutes,' she says, gesturing with her thumb towards the open door of the room behind the shop. It's hard to refuse. I walk to the open doorway, a bit uncertain, and look in. There sits Olav the mechanic on a chair in front of a computer screen with long shining columns of figures. None of them is red, as far as I can see. He has a steaming cup of coffee in one hand and a chocolate bar in the other. He must be twenty years younger than I am, but I'm no longer surprised when I realise that mature men are well below my own age.

'Sit down and relax for a bit,' he says, pouring coffee into a plastic mug and placing it on the table in front of a spare chair and waving me forward as he leans back heavily in his chair. If he gets up as early as I do, and I have a feeling he does, he has been at work for a long time and must be tired. I sit down on the chair.

'Well, how's it going then at The Top?' he says. 'Are you settled in?' My place is called 'The Top' because it has a view over the lake.

'I have been there twice myself,' he says. 'Looking round, and wondering whether to put in an offer. There's plenty of room for car repairing there, but there was so much to be done on the house I thought better of it. I like working on cars, not houses. But maybe it's the other way round for you?' We both glance at my hands. They don't look like the hands of an artisan.

'Not exactly,' I say. 'I'm not much good at either, but given time I will put the house in order. I might need a spot of help now and again.'

What I do, which I have never let anyone know, is I close my eyes every time I have to do something practical apart from the daily chores everyone has, and then I picture how my father would have done it or how he actually did do it while I was watching him, and then I copy *that* until I fall into the proper rhythm, and the task reveals itself and grows visible, and that's what I have done for as long as I can remember, as if the secret lies in how the body behaves towards the task at hand, in a certain balance when you start, like hitting the board in a long jump and the early calculation of how much you need, or how little, and the mechanism that is always there in every kind of job; first one thing and then the other, in a context that is buried in each piece of work, in fact as if what you are going to do already exists in its finished form, and what the body has to do when it starts to move is to draw aside a veil so it all can be read by the person observing. And the person observing is *me,* and the man I am watching, his movements and skills, is a man of barely forty, as my father was when I saw him for the last time when I was fifteen, and he vanished from my life forever. To me he will never be older.

All this would probably be hard to explain to this friendly mechanic, so I merely say:

'I had a practical father. I learned a lot from him.'

'Fathers are great,' he says. 'My father was a teacher. In Oslo. He taught me how to read books, not much else. He wasn't practical, you could not call him that. But he was a fine man. We could always talk. He died a fortnight ago.'

'I didn't know that,' I say. 'I'm sorry to hear it.'

'How could you know? He had been ill for a long time, it was probably the best for him to have it over with. But I miss him, I really do.'

He is just sitting there, and I can see he misses his father, quite simply and straightforwardly, and I would wish it was as easy as that, that you could just miss your father, and that was all there was to it.

I get to my feet. 'I'd better get going,' I say. 'There's this house of mine waiting. I have to keep on with it. Winter's on its way.'

'That's true,' he says, smiling. 'If there's anything you're puzzled about, say the word. We're always here.'

'There is something, in fact. The road up to my house. It's a fair length, you know. When the snow comes it won't be easy for me to keep it clear by hand. And I don't have a tractor.'

'No problem. You can ring this man,' says Olav the mechanic, writing a name and a number on a yellow Post-it—'he's your nearest neighbour with a tractor. He clears his own road and he can easily do yours as well. He is a farmer, and he doesn't have anywhere to go in the morning but down the road and up again. I don't think he'll mind the extra stretch, but he'll likely want something for his trouble. Fifty kroner a time, I would guess.'

'That's reasonable enough. I'll be glad to pay it. Thanks a lot, for your help and the coffee,' I say.

I walk out into the shop and pay for the indicator light bulb, and the mechanic's wife smiles and says, 'Have a good day,' and I go all the way out and get into the car and drive home. The little yellow note I have stuck in my wallet has made the immediate future much less complicated. I feel easy and well and think, Is that all it takes? Anyhow, now winter can come.

Back at The Top I park the car facing my courtyard tree, an ancient almost hollow birch that will come crashing down if I don't do something about it soon, and I go into the kitchen with my shopping bag, fill the kettle for coffee and switch on the percolator. Then I go and get the chainsaw from the shed and a small round file and a pair of ear protectors that were included in the price of the saw. I fetch petrol and two-stroke oil from the garage and place everything on the flagstone in front of the door in the sunlight that feels almost warm now at its height at midday and go in again and find the Thermos and stand by the worktop waiting for the percolator to finish its cycle. Then I fill up the Thermos with steaming coffee and put on warm working clothes and go out again and sit on the flagstone and start to sharpen the saw with the file as gently and systematically as I can until the edge of each tooth in the chain is sharp and shining. I don't know where I learned to do this. Presumably I have seen it on film; a documentary about the great forests or a feature film with a forestry setting. You can learn a lot from films if you have a good memory, watch how people do things and have done them always, but there is not much real work in modern films, there are only ideas. Thin ideas and something they call humour, everything has to be a laugh now. But I hate being entertained, I don't have any time for it.

Anyway, I did not learn how to sharpen a chainsaw from my father, have not watched him doing it and cannot copy him no matter how hard I search my memory. The one-man saws had not reached the Norwegian forests in 1948. There were only a few heavy machines which took five men to carry or had to be transported by horses, and no-one could afford them. So when my father was going to fell the timber on our land that summer so many years ago, it was done in the way it had always been done in those regions: several men at work with a cross-cut saw, and a hatchet, and the air so clean to breathe, and a horse that was trained and a chain-tow to the river where a stack of logs lay on the bank ready and waiting and drying out and the owner's symbol cut into each log, and when all was down that had to be felled and the bark stripped off as good as could be, the logs were rolled out into the water with pike poles by one man at each end of the pile, and then a shout of farewell across the river in words so ancient that no one knew their meaning any longer and the flat splash of water and then gently out into the current, picking up speed and then finally: Bon voyage!

I get up from the flagstone with the newly filed saw in my hand and put it on its side and unscrew the two caps and pour in petrol and fill up with oil and screw the nuts tightly back again. I whistle for Lyra, who comes running at once from some serious digging work behind the house, and with the Thermos under my arm I walk over to the edge of the forest where the dead spruce lies long and heavy and almost white in the heather with no trace of the bark that once covered the whole trunk. After two quick tugs I get the saw going, adjust the choke and let the chain run in the air, there is a howl through the forest, I put the earmuffs on, and then let the saw blade sink into wood. Sawdust spatters my trousers, my whole body vibrates.

6

Back To his youth

THERE WAS THE SCENT of new-felled timber. It spread from the track-side to the river, it filled the air and drifted across the water and penetrated everything everywhere and made me numb and dizzy. I was in the thick of it all. I smelled of resin, my clothes smelled, and my hair smelled, and my skin smelled of resin when I lay in my bed at night. I went to sleep with it and woke up with it and it stayed with me all the day long. I *was* forest. Carrying my hatchet I waded knee-deep in spruce sprigs and cut the branches off in the way my father had shown me; close to the trunk so that nothing would stick out and get in the way of the shaving tool or get caught up in or injure the feet of the man who might have to run on the logs when the floating timber got tangled up and blocked the river. I swung the hatchet to my left and my right in a hypnotic rhythm. It was heavy work, it felt as if everything struck back from every side and nothing would yield by itself, but that did not bother me, I was worn out without realising it, and I just went on. The others had to restrain me, they took me by the shoulders and sat me down on a tree stump and said I had to sit there and rest for a while, but there was resin on the seat of my trousers, and a prickling in my legs, and I rose from the stump with a tearing sound and picked up my hatchet. The sun was baking, my father was laughing. I was like a man intoxicated.

There was Jon's father, and there was Jon's mother for

some parts of the day with her white-blonde hair against
the dark green of the trees on her way up from the boat
with a basket of food, and there was a man called Franz
with a z. He had powerful forearms with a star tattooed
low on the left one, and he lived in a little house beside
the bridge and watched the river rushing by every single
day of the year and knew everything there was to know
about what went on on the water. And there were my father and I, and there was Brona. Jon was not there, they
said he had gone to Innbygda on the bus a few days after
the funeral, but they did not say what he was doing in
Innbygda, and I did not ask. What I was worried about
was whether I would ever see him again.

Jon off To

We started in the morning just after seven and kept
on until evening when we fell into bed and slept like the
dead until we woke with the light and went at it again.
For a time it looked as if we would never get to the end of
those trees, because you can walk along a path and think
that what is around you is a nice little wood, but when
each spruce has to be felled with the cross-cut saw, and
you begin to count, you can easily lose heart and feel certain you will never finish. But when you are in the swing,
and all of you have fallen into a good rhythm, the beginning and the end have no meaning at all, not there, not
then, and the only vital thing is that you keep going until
everything merges into a single pulse that beats and
works under its own steam, and you take a break at the
right time and you work again, and you eat enough but
not too much, and you drink enough but not too much,
and sleep well when the time comes; eight hours at night,
and at least one hour during the day.

I did sleep in the daytime, and my father slept, and

Jon's father and Franz slept, only Jon's mother did not sleep. When it was break time, and we lay down in the heather each under our separate trees and closed our eyes, she went down to the boat and rowed home to Lars to look after him, and when we woke up she was usually back, or we heard the sound of oars from the river and knew she was on her way. Often she would bring with her things we needed, tools she had been asked to fetch or fresh food in the basket, something she had baked and we all enjoyed, and I could not understand how she managed, because she kept at it as hard as any man. And each time I saw my father lying with half-closed eyes glancing at her as she walked towards us, and I did too, I could not stop myself, and because *we* did, Jon's father did as well, in a different way than I had seen him do before, and maybe that was not so strange after all. But I do not think that what we saw was the same thing, for what *he* saw made him embarrassed and apparently surprised. What *I* saw made me want to fell the highest spruce and watch it tip over and fall with a rush and a crash that echoed through the valley and trim it myself in record time and strip it clean myself without stopping even though that was the hardest thing to do and drag it to the river bank with my bare hands and my own back with neither horse nor man to help me and heave it into the water with the strength I suddenly knew I had, and the splash and the spray would rise as high as a house in Oslo.

I had no idea what my father was thinking, but he too put more into it when Jon's mother was there, and of course she often was, so as the days went by we both grew very tired. But he joked and laughed, and then I did the same. We were flying high without really knowing why, at least I didn't know, and Franz was in fine good spirits as well, and with his bulging muscles and peals of laughter he flung out one quip after another as he swung his axe, even once when he was careless and got in the way of a falling tree, and a branch knocked the cap off his head. He dropped his axe and whirled round with a big smile and his hands straight out like a dancer and he cried out:

'I have mixed my blood with Fate and welcome whatever comes with open arms!' And I could picture him standing under the falling tree heavy and almost bursting with heady juices and stopping it dead with his bare hands, the shining blood running from the red star on his forearm. My father scratched his chin and shook his head, but he could not resist smiling.

'Your dad is taking a chance,' Franz said during a break. I sat on a stone by the river rubbing my aching shoulders and looking out over the water, and there he was beside me, saying: 'Your dad is taking a chance felling timber at midsummer and sending it down the river straightaway. It is full of sap, as you may have noticed.' I had noticed, no question, and it made the work harder, because each log had a weight that was roughly double what it would have had at any other time of year, and old Brona could not pull as many as she otherwise would.

'The whole lot might easily sink. The water level is nothing to write home about either, and it's getting lower. I say no more. But if he wants to do it now, then we'll do it now. That's fine by me. He's the boss around here, your dad.'

And he was. I had really never seen him like that before, with other grown men where there was a job to be done, and he had an authority that made other men wait for him to tell them how he wanted things done, and they just went along with what he said as the most natural thing in the world, even though they themselves probably knew better and most certainly had more experience. Until then it had never crossed my mind that anyone except me saw him like that and accepted it, that it was something other and more than a relationship between a father and a son.

The timber pile by the river grew bigger and bigger until we could no longer get the logs onto the top of it, and we started a new one. Brona came down from the upper parts of our wood and turned into position beside the river where we were working, and there was a clanking of chains and the sun sparkling on the water, and the horse was dark and hot and sweating in large patches and smelling strongly as only horses can, and not like anything I had ever experienced in the city. It was a good smell, I thought, and when she stood still there after a lap I could rest my forehead against her flank and feel the stiff coat rub against my skin and just breathe close to that, and there was no need to drive her or even go with her, for after a circuit or two she knew the ropes perfectly. All the same, Jon's father went along, with the reins slack, and my father stood by the river ready with his timber hook as long as a lance in a painting of a tournament in England's age of chivalry. Together they tugged the logs into place as high as they could, and to begin with it was easy, and then it grew harder and harder still, but they would not give up, and eventually it was clear that they had started a competition with each other. When one was about to give up and decided they could go no higher, the other one wanted to go on.

'Come on!' shouted Jon's father, and they each knocked a hook into one end of the log, and my father shouted:

'Heave!'

And Jon's father shouted back:

'Haul away and pull, goddamn it!' And he was scarcely in control, and I realised then that what he was doing was challenging my father's authority, and they took hold and pulled and swayed so that the sweat poured and their shirts slowly turned dark on their backs and the veins stood out on their foreheads and necks and on their arms as blue and broad as the rivers on a map of the world: the Rio Grande, the Brahmaputra, the Nile. Finally there was no way they could go on, and there was no sense to it anyway, we could just as well start a new pile, which would have to be the last one, because we had kept at it for a week, and now we could see the end of the felling and the stacking, and what we had so far accomplished and the amount of timber we had produced, lying shiningly yellow and stripped on the bank, was so awesome to me that I could hardly believe I had been a part of it. But they would *not* stop. They were determined to lift up one more log, and then another, or at any rate one of them was, and which of the two it was seemed to shift. They rolled them up against two logs lying crosswise against the pile, at such an acute angle that they ought to have used ropes, standing on the top and letting the ropes down in two loops around the log and up again like a pulley so that the weight was halved when they came to haul it into place. Franz had shown me how it could be done. But they did not do that, they used only their timber hooks, one on each side, and it was so heavy now that it was getting dangerous, for there were no good footholds and it was virtually impossible for them to do anything in harmony.

It was high time for a rest. I heard Franz call in a mock-desperate voice:

'Coffee! Give me coffee! I'm dying!' from somewhere near the track at the top, and I stood with aching arms, staring at the two grown men who kept pushing each other along, and they groaned aloud in the heat and would not give up, and Jon's mother too came down on her way to the boat and the row home to Lars, and she stopped beside me to watch.

I was aware of her standing there, warm-skinned in her washed-out blue dress, and because she did not go straight to her boat as she usually did, stepping into it and pushing out the oars, I was sure something was going to happen, that it was a sign, and I thought of calling out to my father, telling him to stop all this nonsense he had managed to get himself tangled up in. But I do not think he would have liked that too much, although he often considered my opinion, if I had anything sensible to say, which I often had. I turned to look at Jon's mother, who at this moment had nothing to do with Jon, or maybe that was precisely what she had, but she was in fact two different people and we were equal in height and our hair equally fair after weeks in the blazing sun, but the face that a moment ago had been open, almost naked, was closing now, only her eyes had a dreaming look as if she was not present at all and looking at the same thing that I was looking at, but at something beyond, something larger than this that I could not fathom, but I realised that she was not going to say anything ei-

ther, to stop these two men, that as far as she was concerned they could go on to the bitter end to settle once
and for all something I did not know about, and possibly that was just what she wanted. And that alarmed me.
But instead of letting it drive me off I allowed it to draw
me in, where else was there for me to go? There was nowhere to go, not for me alone, and I took a step closer and
stood right beside her so my hip was almost touching her
hip. I don't think she even noticed, but I felt it like an
electric shock, and the two on the pile noticed, and they
looked down at us and for a second slipped out of their
roles, and then I did something that surprised even me. I
put my arm round her shoulders and drew her close, and
the only person I had done that to before was my own
mother, but this was not my mother. It was Jon's mother,
who smelled of sun and resin as I no doubt did myself,
but also of something more that made me dizzy, just as the
forest made me dizzy and on the verge of tears, and I did
not want her to be the mother of anyone, living or dead.
And the strange thing was that she did not move but let
my arm stay there and leaned lightly against my shoulder,
and I did not know what she wanted, what I wanted myself, but I held her even closer, terrified and happy, and
maybe it was just because I was the nearest one with a
shoulder to lean on, or because I was the son of someone,
and for the first time in my life I did not want to be someone's son. Not to my mother, at home in Oslo, not to the
man on top of the pile so amazed at what he saw that even
though they were in the very middle of hauling and heav-
ing, he straightened up and all but let the timber pole slip
out of his hand and that was distraction enough, and Jon's
father, who looked just as surprised, struggled to hold on.

But he failed and the log swung like a propeller all the way round and struck his ankles before rolling at an angle down the pile, and I *heard* one of his legs break, like a dry twig, before he fell forward shoulder first down the pile and landed on the ground with a thump. It all happened so fast that I did not take it in until he was lying there. I just *looked*. My father stood alone and off balance on the pile with his timber pole swinging from one hand, the river behind him and the blue sky almost white with heat. On the ground Jon's father groaned horribly and his wife, whom a moment before I had held so close and gently around the shoulder, had woken from the trance she was in and torn herself loose and run to her husband. She sank to her knees and bent over him and laid his head in her lap, but she did not say anything, only shook her head as if he had been a naughty boy for the seven hundred and fiftieth time, and she was about to surrender, at least that's what it looked like from where I stood. And for the first time I felt a flash of bitterness towards my father because he had ruined the most complete moment of my life up to then, and suddenly it overwhelmed me, on the brink of rage, my hands shook and I started to feel cold in the heat of the summer's day, and I do not even remember whether I felt sorry for Jon's father, who was so obviously in pain; in the leg that was broken and the shoulder he had fallen on. And then he began to howl. Desolate howling from a grown man because he was wounded and maybe too because one of his sons had just died, and another had left home, perhaps forever, what did he know, and at this moment because everything seemed beyond hope. It was not difficult to understand. But even then I do not think I felt sorry for him, for I was so burstingly full of myself, and his wife only rocked her bowed head, and behind me Franz came running heavily down the path. Even Brona shook her mane and pulled at the reins. From this moment on, I thought, nothing will be as it was.

It had been oppressively warm for several days, and that day was particularly hot. There was something in the air, as they say, it was unbearably humid, our sweat running more freely than normal, and as the afternoon wore on clouds began to gather without any drop in temperature. Before evening the sky was entirely black. But by then we had carried Jon's father across the river in one of the boats and then on to the doctor at Innbygda in one of the two cars in the village, which of course was Barkald's car, and he himself sat at the wheel all through the long drive. Jon's mother had to stay at home with Lars, he could not be left alone for such a long time, and I thought it must be lonely for her and wearisome to be waiting with only the boy and no other grown-up to talk to. What the two men in the car had to say to each other I could not imagine.

When the first flash of lightning struck, my father and I were alone at the table in the cabin looking out the window. We had just eaten, without exchanging a word, and it should really have been daylight, we were still in July, but it was as dark as an October night, and there was a flash and we could see the trees still standing after the felling and the piles on the river bank and the river itself and clear across to the other side. Immediately afterwards there was a crack that made the cabin shake.

'I'll be damned,' I said.

My father turned from the window and looked at me quizzically.

'What did you say?' he said.

'I'll be damned,' I said.

He shook his head and sighed. 'Well, now, you should think of your confirmation,' he said. 'Mind you do.' And then it began to rain, softly at first, but after a few minutes it beat on the roof so that we could hardly hear what we were thinking as we sat at the table. My father leaned back his face to the ceiling as if he could see the water through the panels and the beams and the slates and was hoping that maybe a drop of it might fall on his forehead. He closed his eyes, and it would surely have done us good after that day, to have cold water on our faces. He must have had the same thought because he rose from the table and said:

'What about a shower?'

'I wouldn't say no,' I said. And at once we were in a hurry and jumped up and started to tear our clothes off at full speed and kick them to right and left, and my father ran naked to the wash stand and dipped the soap into the bucket. He looked as odd as I did; sunburned brown from head to navel, and chalk white from the navel down, and he rubbed himself all over until his whole body was covered in whirls of lather, and then he tossed the soap to me, and I did the same as fast as I could.

'Last man out,' he shouted and made for the door. I sprang after him like an American football player to cut off his route and knock him off balance, and he grabbed me by the shoulder to hold me back, but I was so slippery he could not get a hold. He started to laugh and cried:

'You slimy little bugger!' And he could say that, for he had been confirmed a great many years ago, and we got there side by side close together, body to body through the narrow doorway each trying to be first man out and we stopped on the threshold under the eaves and saw water pounding the ground all about us. It was an impressive, almost intimidating sight, and for a moment we just stood there, staring. Then my father took a deep breath and like an actor he screamed:

'It's now or never!' before he leaped out into the rain and started to dance stark naked with his arms in the air and the water splashing onto his shoulders. I ran after him out into the pouring rain to stand where he was standing, jumping and dancing and singing 'Norway in Red, White and Blue', and then he started to sing too, and in no time the soap was rinsed off our bodies and with it the warmth as well, and our bodies were smooth and shining like two seals and probably just as cold to touch.

'I'm freezing,' I called.

'Me too,' he shouted back, 'but we can stand it a bit longer.'

'OK,' I shouted, and slapped my stomach and drummed on my thighs with the flat of my hands to beat some heat into the numb skin until I had the idea of walking on my hands, for I was quite frisky in that way and I shouted:

'Come on, you,' to my father, and bent down and swung up into a handstand, and then he had to follow suit. And we walked on our hands in the wet grass as the rain beat our rumps in a way so icily weird that I had to get back on my feet very soon, but never did anyone have cleaner arses than ours as we ran into the house again and dried ourselves on two large towels and massaged our skin with the coarse cloth to get the circulation going and make the warmth come back, and with a cock of his head my father looked at me and said:

'Well, so you're a man now.'

'Not quite,' I said, for I knew that things were going on around me that I did not understand, and that the grown-ups did understand, but that I was close to being there.

'No, maybe not quite,' he said.

He ran his hand through his hair and with the towel round his hips he went to the stove, tore an old newspaper into strips and twisted them and pushed them into the firebox, then arranged three sticks of firewood around the paper and put a match to it. He shut the door of the stove, but left the ash-pan open for the draught, and the old, tinder-dry wood started to crackle at once. He stayed close to the stove with his arms raised, half bent over the black iron plates and let the rising warmth seep up to his stomach and his chest. I stayed where I was. I looked at his back. I knew he was going to say something. He was my father, I knew him well.

'What happened today,' he said, still with his back turned. 'It was completely unnecessary. The way we were carrying on, it was bound to end badly. I should have stopped it long before. It was in my power, not in his. Do you understand? We are grown men. What happened was my fault.'

I said nothing. I did not know if he meant that he and I

were grown men, or if he and Jon's father were. I guessed the latter.

'It was unforgivable.'

That might be so, I could see that, but I did not like him taking the blame just like that. I felt it was debatable, and if he was to blame, so was I, and even if it felt bad being responsible for such things happening, he belittled me by leaving me out. I felt the bitterness coming again, but milder this time. He turned from the stove and I could read in his face that he knew what I was thinking, but there was no way of discussing it that would make it easier for us. It was too complicated, I could not even think about it any more, not that night. I felt my shoulders sinking, my eyelids dropping, I raised my hands to rub them with my knuckles.

'Are you tired?' he said.

'Yes,' I said. And I *was* tired. Tired in body and tired in mind and weathered in the skin, and I wanted only to lie down under the duvet in my bunk and sleep and sleep until it was not possible to sleep any longer.

He stretched his arm out and tousled my hair, and then he fetched a matchbox from the shelf above the stove and went over and lit the paraffin lamp above the table, blew out the match and opened the door of the stove and threw it into the flames. Our brown-and-white bodies looked probably even funnier in the yellow light of the lamp. He smiled and said:

'You go to bed first. I'll be right behind you.'

But he was not. When I woke up in the night and needed to go out for a pee, he was nowhere to be seen. I walked, drunk with sleep, through the main room, and he was not there, and I opened the door and looked out, and it had stopped raining, but he was not outside either, and when I went back in his bunk was made and neat still in military fashion and looked just the way it had done since the morning before.

7

Now

THE DEAD SPRUCE HAS BEEN TRIMMED and cut up with the chainsaw into manageable lengths about half the size of a chopping block, and I have transported these chunks three at a time in a wheelbarrow and tipped them onto a heap on the ground outside the woodshed, and now they are stacked in a two-dimensional pyramid almost two metres high against the wall under the eaves. Tomorrow the work of splitting them will begin. So far, all is going fine, I am pleased with myself, but this back of mine has had enough for today. Besides, it has gone five o'clock, the sun is down in what must be west, southwest, the dusk comes seeping from the edge of the forest where I was just working, and it is a good time to call a halt. I wipe off the sawdust and the petrol and oil mess sticking to the saw until it is more or less clean and leave it to dry out on a bench in the woodshed, close the door and cross the yard with the empty Thermos under my arm. Then I sit myself down on the steps and pull off my damp boots and rap the wood chips out of them and brush the bottoms of my trousers. I brush my socks, give them a good beating with my working gloves and pick the last bits off with my fingers. They make a nice little heap. Lyra sits watching me with a pine cone in her mouth, it sticks out like an unlit cigar of the really bulky type, and she wants me to throw it so she can chase after it and bring it back, but if once we start on that game she will want to go on and on, and I haven't the energy left.

'Sorry,' I say. 'Some other time.' I pat her yellow head, stroke her neck and gently pull her ears, she loves that. She drops the cone and goes to sit on the door mat.

I leave the boots on the doorstep with their heels against the wall and walk through the hall in my socks to the kitchen. There I rinse out the Thermos in piping hot water from the tap and leave it on the worktop to dry. It is barely two weeks since I had the boiler installed. There had never been one here before. Only a sink on the wall under a cold water tap. I called a plumber who knew my place well, and he told me to dig down to the water pipe in a trench two metres long starting from the outside wall so he could change the angle of the pipe into the kitchen beneath the foundation wall to get it right. And I would have to get on with it, he said, like a bat out of hell, before the frost took hold. The plumber would not do the digging himself, he was not a labourer, he said. I did not mind, but it was heavy work, nothing but gravel and stone all the way down. Some of the stones were really big. It turns out I live on a moraine ridge.

Now I have a dishwashing sink like everyone else. I look at myself in the mirror above the sink. The face there is no different from the one I had expected to see at the age of sixty-seven. In that way I am in time with myself. Whether I like what I see is a different question. But it is of no importance. There are not many people I am going to show myself to, and I only have the one mirror. To tell the truth, I have nothing against the face in the mirror. I acknowledge it, I recognise myself. I cannot ask for more.

The radio is on. They talk about the coming millennium jubilee. They talk about the problems that are bound to crop up in the transition from the solid 97, 98 and 99 to oo on all the computer systems, that we don't know what is going to happen and must safeguard ourselves against potential catastrophes, and Norwegian industry is staggeringly slow to take preventive measures. I cannot make head nor tail of this, and really it does not interest me. The only thing I am certain of is that a whole pack of consultants not one of whom has a clue what is going to happen are out to make a buck. Something they will definitely do and have done already.

I get out my smallest saucepan, scrub some potatoes and put them in, fill up with water and set the pan on the stove. I feel hungry now, working with the wood has sharpened my appetite. I have not felt this hungry for days. I bought the potatoes at the shop, next year I will have my own from the old kitchen garden behind the shed. It is quite overgrown and needs digging up again, but I am sure I can manage that. It's just a matter of putting in the time.

It is important not to be careless about supper when you are alone. It is easily done, boring as it is to cook for one person only. There must be potatoes, sauce and green vegetables, a napkin and a clean glass and the candles lit on the table, and no sitting down in your working clothes. So while the potatoes are boiling I go into the bedroom and change my trousers, put on a clean white shirt and go back to the kitchen and lay a cloth on the table before putting butter into the frying pan to fry the fish I have caught in the lake myself.

Outside, the blue hour has arrived. Everything draws closer; the shed, the edge of the wood, the lake beyond the trees, it is as if the tinted air binds the world together and there is nothing disconnected out there. That's a good thing to think about, but whether it is true or not is a different matter. To me it is better to stand alone, but for the moment the blue world gives a consolation I am not sure I want, and do not need, and still I take it. I sit down at the table feeling well and start eating.

And then there's a knock at the door. The knock as such is not so odd as I do not have a bell, but no-one has put a hand to that door since I moved here, and when people have come to call I have heard the car and gone out onto the steps to greet them. But I have not heard a car, nor have I seen any lights. I get up and leave the meal I have just started, a little annoyed, and go into the hall and open the front door. It is Lars, and behind him in the yard sits Poker, still and for once obedient. The light outside seems almost artificial, as in films I have seen; blue, staged, the source of light invisible, but each thing distinct, and at the same time seen through the same filter, or each thing made of the same substance. Even the dog is blue, it does not move; a clay model of a dog.

'Good evening,' I say, although it is really afternoon still, but in this light it is not possible to say anything else. Standing there, Lars seems embarrassed, or there is something else, something about his face, and with the dog it is the same; a stiffness of the body which they share, and neither of them looks me straight in the eye, they wait, saying nothing, until finally he says:

'Good evening,' and then he goes quiet again, saying nothing about what he wants, and I do not know how to help him.

'I was just about to eat,' I say. 'But that doesn't matter, come in for a bit.' I open the door wide and invite him in, certain that he will refuse, that what he wants to say will

be said there on the steps, if he can only get the words out
he is struggling with. But then he makes up his mind and
takes the last step towards the door, turns to Poker and
says:

'You sit here,' and points to the doorstep, and Poker
walks over to the step and sits down, and I move aside
to let Lars into the hall. I go ahead into the kitchen and
stop by the table where the candles are flickering in the
draught as he follows and closes the door.

'Have you eaten?' I say. 'There's enough here for two,'
and that's more or less true, I always make more than I
need, misjudging my appetite, and the extra portion usually goes to Lyra, and she knows this and is more than
happy when I sit down to eat. She lies by the stove then,
watching me attentively, waiting. Now she gets up from
her place to stand, wagging her tail, sniffing at Lars' trousers. They could do with a wash, no doubt about it.

'Sit you down,' I say, and without waiting for an answer fetch a plate from the corner cupboard and lay it
with cutlery, napkin and glass. I pour him a beer and
help myself too. A few snowflakes on the window and it
would look like Christmas. He sits down, and I can see
him stealing a glance at my white shirt. I do not mind
what he is wearing, the code I follow is for me alone, but
I realise that whatever it was he had come to say, I have
not made it any easier for him. I sit down and urge him to
help himself, and he takes a piece of fish and two potatoes
and a little sauce, and I dare not look at Lyra, for that was
just about what she would have had. We begin to eat.

'That's good,' Lars says. 'Did you catch it yourself?'

'I did,' I say. 'Down by the river mouth.'

'There are plenty of fish there. Perch in particular,' he

says. 'But also pike just by the reeds, and sometimes trout
if you are lucky.' And I nod and go on eating, patiently
waiting for him to get to the point. Not that he would
need a special purpose to come here and have supper. But
finally he takes a big gulp of his beer, wipes his mouth on
the napkin before laying his hands in his lap, and then he
clears his throat and says:

'I know who you are.'

I stop chewing. I think of my face as it was in the mirror just now, does he know who *that* is? Only I know who
that is. Or does he remember the newspapers from three
years ago with me in a big photograph, standing in the
middle of the road in the icy rain, and blood and water
running from my hair and my forehead and down my
shirt and tie, and the glassy, bewildered expression in
my eyes facing the camera, and right behind me, barely
visible, the blue Audi with its rear end in the air and the
front well down the rocky slope. The wet, dark mountain wall, the ambulance with its back doors open and a
stretcher carrying my wife; the police car with its blue
light flashing, the blue blanket round my shoulders, and
a lorry as big as a tank across the yellow centre line, and
rain, rain on the cold, shining asphalt where everything
was reflected double as I was seeing double of everything
in the weeks that followed. All the papers carried that
picture. Perfectly framed by a freelance photographer who
sat in one of the cars that were queueing up in the half-
hour after the crash. He had been on his way to some boring assignment and instead won a prize for the picture he
took in the rain. The low grey sky, the splintered barrier,
the white sheep on the hill behind. All of that in one shot.
'Look this way!' he cried.

But that is not what Lars means. Maybe he has seen one of those pictures, it is entirely possible, but that is not what he means. He has recognised me, as I have recognised him. It is more than fifty years ago, we were just children then, he was ten and I still fifteen and still frightened of everything that went on around me, which I did not understand even though I knew I was close enough to reach out my hand as far as I could, and then maybe reach the whole way and know the meaning of it all. That at least was how it felt to me, and I recall running from the bedroom with my clothes in my hand that summer night in 1948, realising in a sudden panic that what my father said and how things really were, were not necessarily the same, and that made the world liquid and hard to hold on to. A void opened where I could not see over to the other side, and out there in the night, a mere kilometre downriver, maybe Lars lay awake and alone in his bed trying to keep hold of his world, while the shot whose trajectory he could not possibly grasp still filled each cubic metre of air in the small house until he could not hear anything but that shot when people talked to him no matter what they said, and it was the only thing he would hear for a long, long time.

Now more than fifty years later he sits directly opposite me at the table and knows who I am, and I have nothing to say to that. It is not an accusation, though it rather feels like one, nor is it a question, so I do not need to answer. But if I do not say anything it will all get terribly silent and difficult.

'Yes,' I say, looking straight at him. 'I know who you are, too.'

He nods. 'I thought so.' He nods again and picks up his knife and fork and goes on eating, and I can see that he is pleased. That was what he wanted to say. Nothing more, nothing in addition. That, and a confirmation he has now received.

For the rest of the meal I feel slightly ill at ease, trapped in a situation I have not brought about myself. We eat without exchanging many words, just lean forward and glance out the window at the yard where darkness is falling quickly and silently, and we nod to each other and agree that the season with us is in fact the one it is; it gets dark quickly now, doesn't it, and so on, as if that were something new. But Lars seems content and finishes up everything on his plate, and he says almost merrily:

'Thanks very much. It was good to have a proper dinner,' and looks ready to go, and then when he does it is with a light step down the road without the torch, while myself I just feel heavier, and Poker trots along after him towards the bridge and their little cabin and is slowly swallowed up by the night.

I stand by the door a while, listening to the footsteps on the gravel until they too fade out, and a little longer even, and then I hear the faint slam through the dark as Lars shuts his door and see the light come on in the window down there in the cabin by the river. I turn and look around to all sides, but Lars' light is the only light I see. There is a wind starting up, but I stay where I am gazing into the darkness, and the wind rises, it comes rushing from the forest, and I feel cold in nothing but my shirt, I shiver and my teeth start to chatter, and finally I have to give up and go in and shut the door.

I clear the table in the kitchen, two plates on the cloth for the first time in this house. I feel invaded, that's what it is, and not by just anyone.

That's what it is. I fetch Lyra's bowl from the larder and fill it with dry shop-food and carry it back and put it on the floor in front of the wood stove. She looks at me, this is not what she had expected, she sniffs at the food and only slowly starts to eat, swallows each mouthful with demonstrative gloom, and then turns to look at me again, a long look, with those eyes, sighs and goes on, as if she were emptying the poisoned chalice. Spoiled dog.

While Lyra eats I go into the bedroom and take the white shirt off, hang it up on a hanger and pull the working shirt over my head and a sweater and go into the corridor and take the warm pea jacket off its peg and put that on too. Find the torch and whistle for Lyra and go out on the doorstep in my slippers and change into boots. It's blowing hard now. We walk down the road. Lyra first, with me a few metres behind. I can just make out her pale coat, but as long as I can see it, it's like a direction indicator, and I do not switch on the torch, merely let my eyes grow used to the darkness until I stop straining them to catch a light that went out long ago.

When we get to the bridge I stop for a moment where the rails begin and look over at Lars' cabin. The windows are lighted, and I can see his shoulders in the yellow frame and the back of his head without a grey hair yet and the television on at the far end of the room. He is watching the news. I don't know when I last watched the news. I did not bring a television set out here with me, and I regret it sometimes when the evenings get long, but my idea was that living alone you can soon get stuck to those flickering images and to the chair you will sit on far into the night, and then time merely passes as you let others do the moving. I do not want that. I will keep myself company.

We leave the road and go down beside the narrow river on the path I usually take, but I do not hear the water running, the wind soughs and rustles in the trees and bushes about me, and I light the torch so as not to trip on the path and fall into the river because I cannot hear where it is.

When I get to the lake I follow the edge of the reeds until I come to the spot with the bench I have put together and dragged down here, so there is somewhere to sit and watch life at the mouth, see if the fish are jumping and the ducks and the swans that nest here in the bay. They don't do that at this time of year, of course, but they are still here in the morning with the brood they produced in the spring; the young swans as big as their parents now, but still grey and it looks peculiar, like two different species swimming in a line, alike in all their movements, and no doubt they think they are the same, while everyone can see that they are not. Or I can just sit here letting my thoughts fumble vaguely around while Lyra goes through her usual routine.

I find the bench and sit down, but naturally there is nothing to be noticed or to look at right now, so I switch off the light and stay there sitting in the dark, listening to the wind rustling in the reeds with a shrill brittle sound. I can feel how worn out I am after this day, I have kept going for much longer than I usually do, and I close my eyes and tell myself I must not fall asleep now, just sit here for a bit. And then I do go to sleep and wake up all frozen through with the deafening wind around me, and the first thought I have is that I wish Lars had not said what he said, it ties me to a past I thought was well behind me and pulls aside the fifty years with a lightness that seems almost indecent.

I get up from the bench, my body stiff, whistle to Lyra, which is not so easy with numb lips, and then she sits there already close to the bench whimpering softly as she presses her snout against my knee. I switch on the torch. It is blowing massively, there is chaos in the light from the torch when I swing it round, the reeds lie flat on the lake, white foam on the water, and there is a howling sound from the bare treetops bending over and whipping to the south. I crouch down to Lyra and stroke her head.

'Good dog,' I say in English, and it sounds pretty silly, like something from a film I once saw, maybe *Lassie* from the cinema-going of my past, it would not surprise me, or I was dreaming something I have forgotten now, and these words lingered on. It was not from Dickens, though, I cannot recall any 'good dog' in his books, and in any case it is silly. I straighten up again and pull the zip of my jacket up to my chin.

'Come on,' I say to Lyra, 'we're going home,' and she bounds off in sheer relief and storms up the path with her tail in the air, and I follow, not quite that nimbly, my head sunk in my collar and the torch in a tight grip.

8

Back again
to his youth

I CAN CLEARLY REMEMBER that night in the cabin when
my father was not in bed as he had said he would be.
I went out of the bedroom and into the main room and
dressed quickly in front of the stove. As I bent over it,
it was still warm from the evening before and I listened
to the night all around, but there were no sounds that
I could hear other than my own breathing, which was
much too quick and strangely hoarse and heavy in a room
that seemed too large to take stock of although I knew
precisely how many paces there were from wall to wall. I
forced myself to slow my breathing down, drew the air all
the way in and let it carefully out again while I thought:
I have had a good life up to this night, I have never been
alone, not really, and even if my father had been away
for long spells, that was something I had accepted with a
confidence that had been blown away in the course of a
single day in July.

It was a long way off, the blazing hot day, when
I opened the door and went out to the yard in my long
boots. No-one there and almost cool, but not dark now, it
was a summer's night, and above me the clouds split and
opened up as they swept at great speed across the sky, and
the pale light came flickering down so I could easily make
out the path to the river. The water flowed more swiftly
now after the drenching rain, running higher up the
boulders along the banks, and it swelled and rocked with
a faint shine of silver, I could see it from some way off,

and the sound of the river running was the only sound I heard.

The boat was not in its place. I waded a few paces out into the stream and stood there listening for the sound of oars, but there was only the water sweeping round my legs, and I could see nothing either up river or down. The timber piles were there, of course, and their scent was strong in the humid air, and the crooked pine with the cross nailed to its trunk was there, and the fields were there on the other side from the river bank up to the road, but only the clouds in the sky were on the move, and the flickering light. It was a weird sensation to be standing in the night alone, almost the feeling of light or sound through my body; a soft moon or a peal of bells, with the water surging against my boots, and everything else was so big and so quiet around me, but I did not feel abandoned, I felt singled out. I was perfectly calm, I was the anchor of the world. It was the river that did that to me, I could immerse myself in water up to my chin and sit not moving, with the current pounding away and pulling at my body, and remain the person I was, still be the anchor. I turned to look up at the cabin. The windows were dark. I did not want to go back inside again, there was no glow there; the two rooms deserted and empty and the duvets damp and the stove gone out and certainly chillier now than it was out here, I had no business in the cabin now. So I waded ashore and started walking.

First I walked up among the fresh tree stumps to the narrow gravel track behind our land and walked down between the trees to the south instead of north the way we usually did, to where the bridge was and the shop, and it was not hard to find the route now as there were no clouds and the night was light again, like white flour everywhere, a filter I could see quite clearly and maybe touch if I wanted to, and then of course I couldn't. But I tried. I spread my fingers out as I walked between the dark tree trunks, like down a corridor of pillars, and let my hands slide through the air, slowly up and then down again in the powdery light, but I could not feel anything, and everything was as it always was, like any night at all. But life had shifted its weight from one point to another, from one leg to the other, like a silent giant in the vast shadows against the ridge, and I did not feel like the person I had been when this day began, and I did not even know if that was something to be sorry for.

I did not know, and I was too young to look back, so I went on down the gravel path. I heard the river down there beyond the trees, and soon I heard the sounds of the dairy closest to our cabin to the south. It was the cows in the stalls behind the timber walls chewing the cud or lying in the straw, moving from one side to the other in the dark, and they were suddenly quiet, and then they were at it again. Out on the road I could hear the muffled clang of their bells, and I wondered how late it was in the night, whether morning would arrive soon, or whether I could walk down the path to the cow byre and creep inside and sit for a while to feel if it was really warm before I went on. And that is what I did. I just had to go down the path the cows would come up, past the cabin where every- thing was silent and no-one looked out the windows that I could see, and open the door to the dim cowshed and go in. There was a strong smell in there which was good too, and it was as warm as I had imagined it would be. I found a milking stool in the gangway between the gutters and sat down on it by the door I had shut behind me, and I closed my eyes and heard the cows' peaceful breathing behind each stall and their jaws working just as peacefully and the clanking sound of the bells and the creaking of the timbers and the soughing of the night over the roof which was not the wind but the combined hum of all that the night contained. And then I fell asleep.

I woke up feeling someone stroking my cheek. I thought it was my mother. I thought I was a little boy. I have a mother I said to myself, I forgot. And then it came to me what she looked like, feature by feature, until she was almost completely put together and was the one I had always seen, but the face I looked up at was not her face, and for a moment there I was hovering between two worlds with a half-awake eye in each. It was the dairymaid of this farm standing there, which meant it was five o'clock in the morning. I had seen her lots of times and talked to her too. I liked her. She had a voice the sound of a silver flute when she walked up the path to sing the cows home, my father had said raising his hands and holding them slightly to the side of his mouth to demonstrate with fluttering fingers and pouting lips. I did not know what a silver flute sounded like, had never heard anyone play one as far as I knew, but she smiled and looked down at me and said:

'Good morning, lambkin,' and that sounded good to me.

'I was asleep,' I said. 'it was so nice and warm in here.' I sat up with my back straight and rubbed my face with my knuckles. 'You'll need the stool.'

She shook her head. 'No, no, you just stay where you are, I have another one, that'll be fine.' And she walked

down the aisle with a shiny bucket in each hand, found
the other stool and sat down beside the first cow, starting
to wash the pink udder, her skilled hands moving gently.
She had already mucked out and covered the whole floor
with sawdust so it looked clean and pleasant, and now
they were all standing, in two rows: four spotted cows
on each side full of anticipation and milk. She pulled the
pail towards her and took hold just as gently of the teats,
and milk spurted white and jingling against metal, and
it looked so easy, but I had tried several times and never
produced a drop.

I sat watching her with my back against the wall in
the light of the lamp she had hung from a hook beside the
stall; the knotted scarf holding back her hair, the golden
light on her face, her inward-looking gaze and the half
smile, her bare arms, and the bare knees glowing faintly
below her skirts on each side of the pail, and I could not
help it, but inside my trousers I grew tight so suddenly
and with such force I had to gasp for breath, and I could
not even remember thinking about her in that way before.
I held fast to the stool with both hands and felt unfaithful
towards the one I really had on my mind and knew that if
I moved as much as one centimetre now, the least friction
would ruin everything, and she would see it and maybe
hear the helpless whimper in my chest that was already
straining to get out, and then she would know how pa-
thetic I was, and I could not bear that. So I had to think
about other things to ease the pressure, and first I thought
about horses as I had seen them running down the road
through the village, many horses of many colours with
pounding hooves raising the dust on the tinder-dry road,
whirling it up and draping it like yellow curtains between

the houses and the church, but that did not help me a lot, for there was something about the heat of those horses and their curved necks and rhythmic breathing as they galloped along, and all the things about horses that are hard to explain, but you *knew* were there, and then I thought about the Bunnefjord instead. The Bunnefjord at home and the very first swim in the grey-green water in spite of wind and weather on exactly May the first. How cold the water was then, and how the air was knocked out of your body with a gasp when you jumped off the sloping rocks at Katten beach and hit the glassy surface, and you could only jump one at a time because the other one had to stand at the water's edge with a rope acting as lifeguard in case the one in the water got cramps. I was only seven when we decided to do this every single year, my sister and I, not because it was pleasurable but because we felt we had to do something that demanded an extra effort, something that would hurt enough, and this felt suitably painful at the time. Three weeks earlier the German soldiers had arrived in Oslo, and they marched down Karl Johan in an endless column, and it was cold that day and silent in the street, and only the unison crash of boots, like the crack of a whip, beat in among the columns in front of the university building, struck the walls there and bounced back across the cobblestone Universitetsplassen. And then the sudden roar of Messerschmitts sweeping low over the roofs of the city coming in from the fjord, from the open sea and from Germany, and everyone stood silently watching, and my father said nothing, and I said nothing, and no-one in the whole crowd said a word. I looked up at my father, and he looked down at me and slowly shook his head, and then I too shook mine. He

took my hand and led me out of the crowd on the pavement and down the street past the parliament house
to the Østbane Station to see if the bus on Mosseveien
was running or if the south-bound train was on time or
if everything had come to a halt that day except for the
German troops who were all of a sudden everywhere. I
could not remember how we had come into town, if it was
by train or by bus or in someone's car, but somehow we
did manage to get home, and most probably we walked.

Not long after this my father went away for the
first time, and my sister and I started to swim in the
cold fjord, our hearts pounding, the rope at the ready.

It did help to cool me down, thinking about the spring
of 1940, and about my father as he was during those cold
days and the freezing water of the Bunnefjord, from
Katten to Ingierstrand, which were the beaches we went
to, and soon I could loosen my grip on the stool in the
cow byre and stand up without anything going amiss. The
dairymaid had moved on to the next stall and sat there
humming to herself with her forehead against the cow's
flank thinking of nothing but that cow as far as I could
tell, and then I put my stool neatly against the wall and
was about to sneak out of the door and up the path to the
road. But then I heard her voice behind me:

'Would you like a drop?' and I blushed and did not
know why and turned round and said:

'Yes, please, that would be nice,' although I had tried
to avoid fresh milk for a long time. It made my gorge rise
just seeing it in a glass or a cup and thinking about how
warm it was and how thick, but I had slept in her cow
byre and thought about her in a way she did not know

and certainly would not have liked, and I did not see how I could refuse. I took the brimming ladle she passed me and swallowed the whole of it in one gulp. I wiped my mouth hard and waited till I was sure it had all gone down, and then I said:

'Thanks. But I really must go now. My father will have breakfast ready.'

'Yes? That was good and early.' She looked at me calmly as if she knew who I really was and what I was up to, something I was not sure about myself, and I nodded a little too vigorously and turned on my heel and walked away between the stalls and out of the door and had almost reached the road before I had to throw it all up on the ground in front of me. I tore off a few fistfuls of heather and covered up the white vomit with moss so that she would not spot it immediately when she had finished milking and come up the path with the cows, and then maybe feel bad about it.

I followed the road until it narrowed into the track it really was and took a bend towards the river through the tall dewy grass on the level and it ended at a jetty that was almost hidden in the reeds in a backwater here on the east side. I walked onto the jetty and sat at the end of it with my legs dangling over the edge and boots almost in the water, and it was quite light now with the sun on its way up behind the ridge, and through the reeds I could see across to the other side of the river to the farm where Jon lived, or perhaps *had* lived, I did not know any more. They had a jetty too, and there were three rowing boats tied up to it; the one usually used by Jon, and the one I had seen his mother in when she came to the felling. The first was painted blue and the second red, and the third was green and was usually moored by our cabin if some idiot or other had not left it on the wrong bank, and the idiot was me. Now it was here. Someone had built a bench on that jetty, and on the bench sat Jon's mother, and beside her was my father. They were sitting close together. He was shaven, and she had the blue dress on with the yellow flowers that she wore when she went to Innbygda. She had his jacket over her shoulders, and his arm was round her shoulders too as mine had been not twenty-four hours earlier, but he did something that I had not done. He kissed her, and I could see she was crying, but it was not because he kissed her she was crying, and anyway he kissed her, and anyway she cried.

Maybe in those days I lacked a certain type of imagination, and possibly I still do, but what I saw happening on the other side of the river came upon me so unexpectedly that I sat there staring, with my mouth open, not cold, not hot, not even lukewarm, but with my head almost bursting with emptiness, and if anyone had caught sight of me just then, they may well have thought I had run away from a home for backward children.

I could have convinced myself that I was mistaken, that in fact I was not able to see what was happening on the other bank because the river was too wide, and what I thought I dimly saw was a man comforting a woman who had just lost a child and whose husband had been taken to hospital many, many kilometres away, who felt lonely and abandoned. But if that was the case, it was an odd time of day to be doing it, and it was definitely not the Mississippi I sat there staring across, nor the Danube, or even the Rhine, or our own Glomma for that matter, but across this not so very big river that came in a semicircle, crossing the border from Sweden and down through this valley and this village here and back into Sweden some kilometres further south, so it was a moot point whether the water perhaps was really more Swedish than Norwegian, and whether maybe it tasted Swedish if that was possible when you had swallowed some of it. And the river was not even at its widest where I sat on my jetty and they sat on their side.

So I was not mistaken. They kissed each other as if it was the last thing they would do in this life, and I could not watch them, and yet I did, and I tried to think of my mother as a son certainly ought to do when suddenly he came upon something like this, but I could not think about my mother. She slipped away and dissolved and had nothing to do with all this, and then I felt empty again and sat there staring until I could sit there no longer. I stood up slowly, hidden by the reeds and walked over the planks of the jetty as noiselessly as I could and back onto the track and some way along it, and when I turned and looked the two of them were on their feet as well and were walking hand in hand towards the farmhouse.

I did not look back again, just went across the flat field through the tall stalks and round the corner to the place where the path turned into a road and on up past the summer dairy with the cow byre I had slept in. That seemed a long time ago. The light was different now and the air was changed and the sunshine came down over the ridge. It felt nice and warm. There was something in my throat that itched and hurt in a weird way, wanting to come up, but if I swallowed hard I could keep it down. I heard the cows going up the hillside towards the Furu mountain, which was not a real mountain, just a ridge with forest on top, and there were other herds making their way to the best pastures, and bells ringing to right and left.

When I came to the place where the logging had been and the path ran down to our cabin, I stopped and listened. With all the trees gone I had a clear view of the river, and I knew I would hear a boat on its way up. But there was not a sound from that direction. The cabin looked more friendly in this light, and I could easily have gone to it and into the main room and taken the bread out of the bread tin and buttered a slice, for I was hungry now, but instead I went on along the road towards the bridge and the shop. It took me twenty minutes. Franz's house stood on a rise close to the river just this side of the bridge. From the road I could see his door open and the sun shining into the hallway. I heard the sound of music from a radio. I just walked down the gravel path right up to the entrance, took the three steps up and called in through the doorway:

'Hello! Any breakfast going here?'

'Hello, yes! Get the hell in here!' was the answer from inside.

9 Now

THE GALE ROARS ALL NIGHT. I wake up several times and hear the wind humming along the walls and more than that; it takes so fierce a hold of the house that the old timbers groan; sounds come from all sides, shrill, whistling, almost threatening sounds from the forest out there and metallic rattling and a powerful crash from somewhere I reckon must be close to the shed, and it does worry me a bit as I lie in the dark with my eyes open looking up at the ceiling, but it's warm under the duvet, and I have no intention of getting up now. And then I wonder whether the slates will hold as they are meant to or whether soon they will fly off the roof and whirl across the yard and maybe hit my car and dent it. I decide that probably they will not and go back to sleep.

Next time I wake up it is possibly blowing still harder, but now like a sucking where the wind is being ploughed and split by the roof ridge; no rattling, no crashing, more like a booming in the depths of a ship near the engine, for everything is rocking now in the darkness and moving onward, and the house has masts and lanterns, and a foaming wake and is dressed all over, and I like that, I like being on a ship, and maybe I am not so wide awake after all.

It is half past seven when I open my eyes for the last time. That is late by my standards, far too late. There is just a hint of grey light in the window and all is strangely quiet on the other side of the glass. I lie there without moving and listen. Not a creak from the world out there, only the padding of Lyra's paws and claws on her way across the kitchen floor to her water bowl. The universe has been almost bursting with sound, and now it has gone flat. All that is left is one patient dog. I can hear her loudly drinking and swallowing, and then she utters a low, discreet piping sound that says she would like to go out to do what she cannot do indoors. If it is not too much bother.

I sense that my back is not too good and roll over onto my stomach and push myself over the edge of the bed with my knees down on the floor first and then raise myself tentatively into a standing position. That goes well, but I am really stiff and sore after yesterday's efforts. I go barefoot into the kitchen, past the dog and into the hall.

'Come on, Lyra,' I say, and she pads after me. I open the outer door and let her out into the semi-darkness. Then I go back and dress, open the woodbox, which fortunately is full of logs, and light the stove as systematically as I can. I never succeed at the first try, something my father always did, but as long as there is time it will burn in the end. My sister could never do it. She would have plenty of dry wood at her disposal, and strips of newspaper and a stove that drew well, and nothing would ever burn except the paper. 'How can a housefire even start? Can you tell me that?' she asked. I miss my sister. She too died three years ago. Of cancer. There was nothing to be done, she was diagnosed far too late. As time passed she and my wife became good friends. They would often chat on the phone in the evenings commenting on the affairs of the world. Sometimes I was the subject of their discussion and they would laugh themselves helpless over 'the boy with the golden trousers', as they called me. You've always been the boy with the golden trousers, you can't deny that, they said, laughing. I think it was my sister who used the nickname first. I did not mind, there was never any malice in their laughter, they just had a sense of humour and wanted to tease me. I have always been pretty serious myself, but you can overdo that too. And they were right enough, I have been lucky. I have said that before.

In the course of one month they both died, and after they were gone I lost interest in talking to people. I really do not know what to talk to them about. That is one reason for living here. Another reason is being close to the forest. It was a part of my life many years ago in a way that nothing later has been, and then it was absent for a long, long time, and when everything around me suddenly turned silent, I realised how much I had missed it. Soon I thought of nothing else, and if I too were not to die, at precisely that point in time, I had to go to the forest. That's how it felt, and that simple. It still is.

I switch the radio on. It is halfway through P2's morning news. Russian grenades are pouring down on Grozny. They are at it again. But they will never win, not in the long run, that goes without saying. Tolstoy knew that already in *Hadji Murat,* and that book was written a hundred years ago. It is really incomprehensible that the great powers cannot learn the lesson that in the end it is they themselves who will disintegrate. But of course the whole of Chechnya can be demolished. That is rather more possible today than a hundred years ago.

The stove is crackling well. I open the bread box and cut a couple of slices, put water on to boil for coffee and then I hear Lyra give her short sharp bark on the steps. It is her way of ringing the bell and is easy to distinguish from the other sounds she makes. I let her back in. She goes to lie down by the stove where warmth is gradually spreading. I lay a breakfast table for myself and prepare Lyra's in her bowl, but she must wait her turn. I am the boss. I eat first.

Day is coming now, over there by the forest. I lean forward and look out the window, and I am more than a little dumbfounded at what I see in the morning light. My yard tree, the big old birch, has been knocked down by the gale and lies huge and almost unreal between the shed and my car; the topmost branches practically reaching to the kitchen window, other branches on top of the roof rack of the car, and others again have torn the gutter off the shed and bent it into a large V so that it hangs down and bars the door to the woodshed. It's a good thing I have filled up the woodbox.

That explains the thud from last night. Automatically I get to my feet, about to go out, but of course there is no sense in that. That birch is not going anywhere. So I sit down again and go on with my breakfast, looking out the window while I try to think out a plan for the removal of this giant that has lain down to rest in my yard. First I must rescue the car, that's obvious, and then move it away. Then the branches, the ones in front of the woodshed, too, to see if it is possible to get in there. I must have firewood, and I must have a car to drive. That is vital. The chainsaw will need filing again, there is no way around it after yesterday's work, and I may need more petrol and two-stroke oil, it will have to be checked, and in which case I must drive for more, but the car is probably trapped. I feel a touch of panic and cannot understand why. This is no crisis. I am here of my own choice. I have plenty of food in the fridge and water in the tap, I can walk as far as I please, I am fit and well, and I have all the time in the world. Or do I? It does not feel like that. It does not feel like that at all. It suddenly feels claustrophobic. I could die at any minute, that's the way it is, but this is something I have known the last three years, and not given a damn and still do not. I look at the birch. It just about fills the whole yard and is so huge it overshadows everything. I get quickly up from the table and go into the bedroom and lie down on the bed with my clothes on, which is contrary to all my rules, and I gaze up at the ceiling and my head is churning like a roulette wheel, and the ball hops from red to black to red again and finally comes to rest in one bowl, and of course it is the one for the summer of 1948, or more precisely the day that summer was over. I stood under the oak tree in front of the shop and looked up and saw the light swirling through the rushing leaves as the wind came up and dropped again, and it blinded me in small flashes and made me blink hard and the tears started to flow, and I closed my eyes and felt red heat on my eyelids and heard the river behind me as I had heard it each day for almost two months, and I wondered what it would be like when now I would not hear it any more.

It was hot under the oak. I felt tired. We had got up early that morning and had breakfast almost without talking, and then walked from the cabin up the gravel track to the bridge and past Franz's house where the sun was shining in through the open door, in a bright shaft across the rag rug and slanting along one wall, but he himself was nowhere to be seen, and I felt sad that I had missed him.

The bus was waiting in the sun, vibrating from the running diesel engine. I was leaving the village and making the long trip home to Oslo, changing to the train at Elverum. My father stood close behind me in front of the shop on the square with his hand on my head, and he lightly rumpled my hair and bent down and said:

'You'll be fine. You know where to get off at Elverum Station, and from which side the train leaves, and at what time,' and he carried on like that with more details, and all this he said as if it really did mean something, as if at fifteen I could not make the journey alone without instructions. Actually I felt much older, but I had no way of showing it that I could think of, and if I had, it would not be anything that he could accept.

'This summer has been quite something,' he said. 'We can surely agree on that.' He stood behind me still with his hand on my head, but he did not ruffle my hair any more, just gripped so tight it almost hurt, and I do not think he realised, and I did not say anything to make him let go. He bent forward again and said:

'But that's life. That's what you learn from; when things happen. Especially at your age. You just have to take it in and remember to think afterwards and not forget and never grow bitter. Do you understand?'

'Yes,' I said aloud.

'Do you understand?' he said, and I said yes again and nodded, and then he realised how hard he was gripping my hair and let go with a little laugh which I could not make out, I did not see his face. And I heard what he said, but I did not know if I had understood. How could I? And I did not understand why he used those exact words, but I have thought it over a thousand times since, because in the next moment he turned me round with a light hold on my shoulder, and ran his hand through my hair once more, looked at me almost squintingly and with that half smile at his mouth I liked so much he said:

'Now you're going to get on this bus and then change to the train at Elverum and it will take you home to Oslo, and then I will finish up here, and when that's done I'll be right behind you. OK?'

'Yes,' I said. 'OK.' And there was an icy feeling in the pit of my stomach, for it was *not* OK. I had heard those words before, and the vital question I have put to myself again and again during the time that followed is whether something happened he could not control, or whether he knew already then that he would never follow me. That this was the last time we saw each other.

I boarded the bus, of course, and I sat down with my rucksack on my lap and turned to stare out of the bus window at the shop and the bridge over the river and my father standing there tall and dark and lean in the flickering shadows under the oak tree and at the sky which had never been wider or deeper blue than in that summer of 1948 over precisely that village, and then the bus moved in a big semicircle out to the road. I pressed my nose against the glass and gazed into the cloud of dust slowly rising outside and hiding my father in a whirl of grey and brown, and I did everything you are *supposed* to do in a situation like that, in such a scene; I rose quickly and ran down the gangway between the seats to the last row and jumped up on it knees first and placed my hands on the window and stared up the road until the shop and the oak tree and my father had vanished round a bend, and all this as if I had been thoroughly rehearsed in the film we have seen so often, where the fateful farewell is the crucial event and the lives of the protagonists are changed forever and take off in directions that are unexpected and not always nice, and the whole cinema audience knows just how it will turn out. And some cover their mouths with their hands, and some sit chewing their handkerchief with tears running down their cheeks, and some swallow in vain to get rid of the lump in their throat while they squint at the screen dissolving into a jumble of colours, and others again are in such a fury they almost get up and leave because they have experienced something like this in their own life which they have never forgiven, and one of *those* jumps up from his seat in the dark and shouts:

'You damn prick!' at the figure under the oak tree now showing against the back of his head, and he does it on behalf of himself and on behalf of me, and I do thank him for his support. But the point is that I did not know how things would turn out that day. No-one had told me! And there was no way I could know what lay behind the scene I myself had just been through. I just kept running up and down between my seat and the window at the back with a sudden, directionless alarm in my body, and I sat down and stood up again and walked up and down the gangway and sat in a different seat and left that too, and I went on like this the whole time I was alone on the bus. I saw the driver's eyes in the front mirror watching me and at the same time manoeuvring the vehicle along the winding dirt road, and it obviously frustrated him, but he could not stop watching, and he did not say anything at all. And then two families got on at a stop halfway to Innbygda, where the river took a bend and disappeared into the forest towards Sweden, and they had children and dogs and bags in tow, and one lady had a hen in a cage, and it cackled and cackled, and then I forced myself to sit still on my seat and finally I fell asleep with the rattling window banging against my head and the drone of the diesel engine singing in my ears.

Now

I open my eyes. My head feels heavy on the pillow. I have been asleep. I raise my hand and look at my watch. Only half an hour, but it is unusual. After all, I had only just got up, and late too. Was I *so* worn out?

It's broad daylight outside. I sit up with a jerk as I swing my legs over the edge of the bed, and then I suddenly feel so dizzy that I fall forwards and cannot stop, there is a flash behind my eyes as I flop down, one shoulder first. I hear myself give a strangely loud groan when I hit the floor. And there I am. In pain too. I'll be damned. I breathe cautiously, making as little effort as possible. It isn't easy. It is too soon for me to die. I am only 67, I am fit. I go walking with Lyra three times a day, I eat healthily, and I have not smoked for twenty years. That should do it. In any case I do not want to die like this. I should have made a move by now, but I dare not try, because I might not be able to, and what then? I do not even have a telephone. I have postponed that decision, do not want to be accessible. But then obviously others are not accessible to me either, I admit that. Especially at this moment.

I close my eyes and lie quite still. The floor is cold against my cheek. It smells of dust. I hear Lyra breathing by the stove in the kitchen. We should have been for a walk long ago, but she is patient and does not nag. I feel a bit sick. That should tell me something. It tells me nothing. I just feel sick. Then I get irritated and squeeze my eyes hard shut to fix my gaze inwards and roll round until my knees are beneath me and with one hand on the doorframe I ease myself carefully up. My knees are shaking, but I succeed. I keep my eyes shut tight until any hint of dizziness has gone, and then I open them and look straight down at Lyra, who stands before me on the kitchen floor with those clever eyes looking attentively up into mine.

'Good dog,' I say without feeling stupid. 'Now we'll go out.'

And that's what we do. I go into the hall, my legs shaking slightly, and put my jacket on and button it up without too much trouble and go out onto the doorstep with Lyra at my heels and put on my boots. And with great attention I listen to my own body to find out if anything has gone amiss in the fincly tuned machinery which even an old body is, but it's not easy to know for sure. Apart from a faint feeling of sickness and a sore shoulder, everything seems normal. Maybe a little more light-headedness than usual, but that's probably not so strange now I am on my feet after having been out for the count.

I try not to look at the birch, and that is difficult, as there are not many other places to fix my gaze whichever way I turn, but I squint and walk close to the house wall avoiding the longest branches and have to bend one out of the way and then another one, and slip through to the drive and with my back to the yard I start out on the road down to the river and Lars' cabin with Lyra in a yellow dance in front of me along the road. I turn into the path by the bridge and walk along the stream until I stop on the bank close to the river mouth. November, and I can see the bench where I sat yesterday evening in the windy darkness and two pale swans on the grey water of the bay and the bare trees against a pale morning sun and the dull green forest on the other side of the lake in a milky mist to the south. A quite unusual stillness, like Sunday morning when I was small, or Good Friday. A snap of the fingers like a pistol shot. But I can hear Lyra breathing behind me, and the pale sunshine cuts my eyes, and then I suddenly feel really sick and stand bent over on the path throwing up onto the withered grass. I close my eyes, my head is spinning, I am not well, dammit. I open my eyes again. Lyra stands looking at me, and then she comes up to sniff at what I have got rid of.

'No,' I say, unusually sharp. 'Back off,' and she turns quickly and runs on along the path, and she stops and looks back with her tongue lolling.

'All right,' I say. 'All right. We'll go on.'

I start walking again. The nausea has lessened, and if I take it easy I will make it round the lake. Or will I? I am not sure. I wipe my mouth with a handkerchief and the sweat from my forehead and go right on to the edge of the reeds and slump down on the bench. So I'm sitting here again. A swan comes in to land. Soon there will be ice on the lake.

I close my eyes. Suddenly I remember a dream I had last night. That is strange, it was not there when I woke up, but now it is perfectly clear. I was in a bedroom with my first wife, it was not our own bedroom, we were in our thirties, I am sure of that, my body felt that way. We had just made love, I had performed as well as I could, which was usually more than good enough, at least I thought so. She lay in bed and I stood by the chest where I could see my whole body in the mirror except for my head, and I looked good in the dream, better than I really did. She flung the duvet aside and was naked, and she looked good too, really beautiful, almost unfamiliar in fact, and not quite like the woman I had just made love to. She looked at me the way I had always feared and said:

'You're only one of many, of course.' She sat up, naked and heavy in the way I knew, and she filled me with disgust right up into my throat and at the same time with terror, and I shouted:

'Not in *my* life, I'm not,' and then I started to weep, for I had known that this day would come, and I realised that what I was most afraid of in this world was to be the man in Magritte's painting who looking at himself in the mirror sees only the back of his own head, again and again.

II

10

FRANZ AND I WERE IN THE KITCHEN of his small
house on the rock by the river. The sun came in
through the window shining whitely down on the table
where we sat each with a white plate and a white cup of
brown coffee poured from the brightly polished kettle on
the stove he always kept burning, both summer and winter, he said, but in summer he had the windows open. The
kitchen was painted the blue colour which was custom-
ary out here, it kept the flies away, was the saying, and
that was probably right, and he had made all the furni-
ture himself. I felt good in that room. I picked up the jug
and poured a little milk into my cup. That made the coffee
smoother and more like the light and not so strong, and
I shut my eyes into a squint and looked across the water
flowing past below the window, shining and glittering
like a thousand stars, like the Milky Way could sometimes do in the autumn rushing foamingly on and winding through the night in an endless stream, and you could
lie out there beside the fjord at home in the vast darkness
with your back against the hard sloping rock gazing up
until your eyes hurt, feeling the weight of the universe
in all its immensity press down on your chest until you
could scarcely breathe or on the contrary be lifted up
and simply float away like a mere speck of human flesh in
a limitless vacuum, never to return. Just thinking about
it could make you vanish a little.

I turned round and saw the red star Franz had on his

forearm. It was glowing in the sunlight and waving like a flag each time he moved his fingers or clenched his fist. He often did. He was probably a communist. Many lumberjacks were, and with good reason, my father had said.

This is what Franz told me.

It was 1942. My father came from the north through the forest, searching for a place where he could take cover close to the border when he had to go to Sweden with papers and letters and sometimes films for the Resistance, and later return to when his mission was completed and his tracks obliterated, a place he could use numerous times. He was in no hurry. He was not on the run then, or he did not behave as if he was. He made no attempt to hide and was open and friendly to everyone he came across. What he needed was a place where he could think, he said, and for some reason no-one doubted that explanation. He came from *inthere*. Have you been *inthere*? they said, when someone came home and on rare occasions had been to the capital. People were different there. Everyone knew that. So it made sense. He wanted to have a place where he could think. Others could think where they happened to be at the time. Nothing to make a fuss about.

Only Franz had any idea of what he really wanted the place for. The two of them knew about each other from earlier, but they had not met until the day my father walked up the steps to Franz's door and knocked and spoke the pre-arranged words:

'Are you coming? We're going out stealing horses.'

I turned from the window and stared at Franz and said:

'*What* did you say he said?'

'He said: "We're going out stealing horses." I don't know who thought that up. Your father himself, probably. Not me, anyway. But I knew what he was going to say. The message had come by bus from Innbygda.'

'Oh,' I said.

'I took to him at once, I did,' said Franz.

And who would not? Men liked my father, and women liked my father, I knew of no-one who did not like him, except maybe Jon's father, but that was about something else, and I imagined that under different circumstances they would really not have had anything against each other at all, and might well have been friends. And the strange thing is that it was not as I have seen it so many times later in life, that someone who is so well liked by so many people can often be a touch shapeless and unassuming and will go out of their way not to provoke. My father was not like that at all, it is true he smiled and laughed a lot, but he did that because it came to him naturally and was not something he did to satisfy anyone's need for harmony. Not mine, anyway, and I liked him a lot, although he sometimes made me feel shy and that was probably because I did not know him as a boy ought to know his father. During the past years he had often been away, and with the Germans in our country, months could pass when I did not see him, and when finally he came home and walked the streets like any other man, he was different in a way it was hard for me to pinpoint. But each time he came home he had changed a little, and I had to concentrate hard to hold on to him.

Nevertheless I never doubted my special place in his heart, nor my sister's, though mine maybe even more spe-

cial than hers because I was a boy and he was a man, and
it never occurred to me that I was not on his mind both
often and long when we were not in the same place. As
when he came to this village in 1942, and I was at home
in the house we lived in beside the Oslo fjord and went to
school every day and sat there dreaming of journeys we
would make together once the Germans were beaten and
had left for good, while he was out hunting for a place
where he could think, as he put it, and use as a hiding
place and a base for his trips across to Sweden with papers
and sometimes films for the Resistance.

It was Franz himself who showed my father the summer cabin that was vacant after a foreclosure before the
war and since then had been empty for four years. Barkald
had stepped in and bought the smallholding it belonged
to, for a song naturally, so he was in fact the owner of the
property. It was of no use to him. He let it slide, the cow
byre had collapsed already, but then there was no herd to
fill it with, and my father took a liking to the place at once.
Especially because it was on the east bank of the river
with a twenty-minute walk to the nearest bridge, and because there was no other building behind the farmsteads,
not even a hut, until you were way beyond the Swedish
side of the border. But that was not all. Franz believed my
father enjoyed being there. Enjoyed doing the things that
were necessary to make everything he was doing look le-
gitimate and had to be done anyway; cutting the grass,
clearing up the remains of the byre and burning them, fix-
ing the roof tiles, cleaning the scrub from the river bank,
repairing the roof and renewing the gable boards on the
house, exchanging new panes for the old broken ones in

the windows. He mended the stove with oven-sealer. He swept the chimney. He made two new chairs. All these were things that came easily to him, which he never had the time nor the freedom to do in Oslo where we rented three rooms and a kitchen on the second floor of a large three-storey Swiss chalet next to Ljan Station with a view of inner Oslofjord and the Bunnefjord.

He had not intended his stays to be long, just enough to make people grow accustomed to seeing him on the other side of the river, climbing over the roof or pottering around the yard or sitting on one of the rocks by the river thinking, as he put it, because he had to be close to water to do that. That too was a bit odd, of course, but nothing to argue about either, and they could see him when he walked across Barkald's meadow with the empty bag over his shoulder on his way to the shop about the time the bus came from Innbygda and Elverum, or they saw him on the way back with his supplies and maybe other things. But every time he had been to Sweden to deliver what there was to deliver to the person expecting it, and came back across the border under cover of night, he found several more things he could put in order or improve on before he went back to Oslo. So then he stayed a bit longer and cut the grass once more or before leaving made good the masonry around the chimney, for it had cracked from top to bottom and might collapse and send some tiles flying onto someone's head, and in that way he made himself in a couple of years an alternative life that we, his family in Oslo, knew nothing about. Not that this was the way I thought about it when Franz and I sat in his kitchen, and he talked to me about my father, who had established himself in Barkald's decrepit small farmstead more than five years earlier to provide himself with a cover for the last link of a courier line to Sweden in the second year of the war in Norway, and started up what they called 'the traffic'. It was not until many years later I realised that this was what it must have been like for him. He spent as much time in the village by the river as he did with us beside the Bunnefjord. But that we did not know and were not supposed to know; that there was one place only and where that place was. We never knew where he was. He went away, and then he came home again. One week later, or one month, and we became used to living without him, from one day to another, from one week to another. But I thought about him constantly.

All this that Franz talked about was news to me then, but I had no reason to doubt anything he said. Why *he* should tell me about those times, when my father had never done so, was a question I sat pondering while he talked on, but I did not know whether I could ask him that and have an answer I could live with, for he must certainly have thought I knew all about it already and was merely amused to hear another version. I wondered too why my friend Jon or his mother or his father or the man at the shop I spoke to so often or Barkald or whoever the hell else had not mentioned to me that only four years earlier my father had been in the village so often, although on the other side of the river where the summer cabins were, that he could almost be considered a resident. But I did not ask that.

There was a German patrol stationed permanently on the farm nearest to the church and the shop. They had just requisitioned the farmhouse and pushed the whole family out into the pensioner's cottage where it was crowded already, and often but not always there was a guard on the gravel approach to the bridge over the river. He carried a sub-machine gun on a strap over his shoulder and a cigarette in his mouth when his officers were not watching. Sometimes he actually sat down on a rock with the machine gun on the ground in front of him, took his helmet off to give his flattened hair a long and good scratching, smoking and gazing down between his knees and his shiny boots until the cigarette had burned right down to his fingers, and he could barely bring himself to stand up again. Behind him the river rushed down the rapids, its tone unchanging, as far as he could tell, and they were bored here, nothing happened, the war was elsewhere. But it was better than the Eastern front.

When my father decided to take that route, across the bridge, past Franz's house and down the narrow gravel track on the east side of the river, he stopped first for a chat with the German guard, for he was quite good at German, many people were in those days, it was a language you had to learn at school whether you wanted to or not until well into the Seventies. It was not the same guard every time, but they all looked so much like each other that few could see any difference, and anyway not many were interested and instead tried to act as if they did not exist, and what German the people had learned was suddenly forgotten. But my father soon found out where each of them came from, whether they had wives in Germany, whether they preferred football or athletics or maybe swimming, whether they missed their mothers. They were ten or fifteen years younger than him and sometimes more, and he talked to them in a considerate way, something not many others did. Franz could see from his window my father standing in front of the man in the grey-green uniform, or the boy almost, and they offered each other a cigarette, and one lit up for the other according to which of them was treating and held the match in his hollowed hand even when there was no wind, and they bent their bodies in an intimate arc above the small flame, and if it was evening their faces were lit with a yellow shine and they stayed there on the gravel in the still air talking and smoking until their cigarettes were down to the butts and stubbed out on the gravel each beneath his boot, and then my father raised his hand and said *'Gute Nacht'* and was given a grateful *'Gute Nacht'* in return. He walked across the bridge smiling to himself and on down the road to the cabin with the shabby bag on his back and what was in that bag. And he knew that if he did something unexpected, like suddenly turning and starting to run, the German boy would quite certainly snatch his machine gun quick as lightning from his shoulder and shout: 'Halt!', and if he did not stop then he would have a salvo of bullets coming at him and perhaps be killed.

At other times he walked along the main road with a slightly fuller bag and turned into the meadows along Barkald's fence and rowed across the river. He waved to people he saw, either German or Norwegian, and no-one stopped him. They knew who he was; he was the man who was putting Barkald's cabin back in shape, they had asked Barkald and he confirmed the assignment, and they had been out to the place three times and found a quantity of tools and two books by Hamsun, *Pan* and *Hunger*, which they could happily accept, but they never found anything suspicious. He was the man who at regular intervals took the bus out of the village and stayed away for a good while, for he was working on several similar projects, and there was nothing wrong with his certificate of border residency nor his other papers.

My father kept the line going for two years, through summer and winter, and when *he* was not at the cabin someone from the village made the final leg across the border; Franz once or twice, and Jon's mother when she could get away, but there was considerable danger involved, for everyone in the district knew each other and each other's routines, and anything out of the norm was observed and taken down for later use in the log book we keep of each other's lives. But then he came back, and those who were supposed to be ignorant of the traffic still were. Myself, among others, and my mother and my sister. Sometimes he fetched the 'mail' himself straight off the bus, or from the shop both before and after closing time, at other times it was Jon's mother who picked it up and took it with her when she rowed up the river with food that Barkald often asked her to cook, because the handyman must be fed or so it had to appear, as if he could not cope with a cooking stove on his own but had to have a woman's assistance. It was a bit strange, I thought, that he would need help with that, when he could turn his hand to most things. He was really just as good a cook as my mother, when the need arose, I knew that, I had seen it and tasted it numerous times, only he was slightly lazier over that sort of thing, so when he and I were on our own we ate what we called

'simple country food'. Fried eggs, most often. I had nothing against that. When it was my mother in the kitchen
we were served what she called 'proper meals'. When we
had money, that is. It was not always so.

But Jon's mother rowed up the river once or twice
a week, with food or without it, with 'mail' or without it, to act as some kind of cook for my father so
he could dig in to some proper meals and not fall ill
and weak because of the unbalanced diet men who
live alone generally swear by and not be fit enough
to carry out the work he was meant to do. At least that
was the way Barkald told it when he was at the shop.

Jon's father did not take part. He was not against what
they were doing, he had never said as much that anyone
heard, at least Franz had not, but he would have nothing to do with the 'traffic'. Every time something was
about to happen he looked the other way, and he looked
the other way when his wife went down to the river carrying her basket and stepped into the red-painted boat to
row up to my father. He even looked the other way when
a strange man with his arms around a tightly lashed suit-
case and a city hat on his head was silently shown into
his barn at twilight to sit there alone on a cartwheel, confused and silent in his inappropriate clothes, waiting for
dark. And when the same man was taken by boat upriver
in the night, all without a sound, first across the yard and
then down to the jetty where not a word was uttered,
not a light lit, he did not comment on that either, neither
then nor later, even if the man was the first of several, for
now not only 'mail' passed through the village on its way
across the border to Sweden.

And it was late autumn and there was snow, but no ice on the water anywhere, and you could still row on the river. And that was a good thing, because early one morning before the rooster fell off his perch, as Franz put it, a man in a suit was dropped off on the main road in the dark and walked with his bag on his back through the snow up the farm road and straight into Jon and his family's yard. The man wore summer shoes with thin soles, and was half dead with cold in his wide trousers, his legs shaking, making his trouser legs roll and sway from his hips down to the light shoes when Jon's mother went out onto the doorstep with a shawl round her shoulders and a blanket under her arm. It was an odd sight, she told Franz when she came back from Sweden in May of '45, almost like a circus act. She gave him the blanket and showed him over to the barn where he had to stay in the hay through all the hours of the white day until evening came, for about twelve hours, because the light was all gone around five o'clock, and it had been five when he came walking up the road. But the man could not take it. He went nuts in there, Jon's mother said, at two o'clock he cracked and went berserk. He started yelling the strangest things, picked up an iron bar and struck out and pounded around him so that flakes showered down off the roof poles and several of the lathes in the haycart were knocked straight off. He could easily be heard from the yard outside, and maybe they heard him upriver, for the air was still and carried his cries clearly across the water, or they heard him right down on the road where the Germans drove by at least two or three times a day trying to be as alert as they could. And then the animals in the byre alongside grew restive. Bramina whinnied and kicked out at the walls of her stall and the cows mooed in their stalls as if spring had come and they longed to go out to pasture, and something had to be done pronto.

He had to leave that barn. He had to be sent upriver without a moment's delay. But it was daylight still and easy to see far across the fields and through the bare trees with the snow on the ground making everything visible in clear silhouette, and along the first stretch you could see the river from the road. But he had to go. Jon had not yet come back from school and the twins were playing in the kitchen. She heard them laughing and rolling on the floor, having mock fights as they always did. She quietly put on warm clothes, cap and mittens and went down the steps and across the yard to the barn as her husband woke up on the divan and rose to his feet, and I may be laying it on a bit here and cannot be sure of this, but still I am convinced that a strange creature like a ghost had come into the house that pulled him up and jerked him out into the hall where the naked bulb hung that was never turned out so it would shine out of the small window to help people find their way through the dark of the night, and the picture of his father hung there with his long beard in a gold frame above the coat pegs, and on his shoeless feet he stood there dazed, where the door opened outwards as it was meant to do so the snow would not beat in when the weather was wild, and *now* he did not want to look any other way at all but instead was staring after her. Behind her back she sensed him standing there and it surprised her in an intimidating way, but she did not turn round, merely pulled the bar off the lock and opened the big barn door and went in and stayed there for an eternity. He stood where he was, staring. She came out at last with the stranger in tow, she had her warm boots on and her jacket and he was wearing the suit and his summer shoes, with the grey bag on his back. He had a jumper on now under the suit, and it made his jacket too tight and bulky and he looked pretty inelegant. He no longer had any weapon, and she practically led him by the hand, as he was humble now, and almost limp and loose-jointed and maybe exhausted after an outburst he had not expected. Halfway across the yard on the way past the house towards the jetty she suddenly turned and looked back. Their footprints were obvious in the snow, first the stranger's tracks up the farm lane, and then her own from the house, and finally both sets from the barn to the point where they were standing now. The impressions of the urban summer shoes were striking and unlike any others you would see in those parts at this time of year, and she looked down at the ground, thinking hard and biting her lip, as the man grew restive and began to pull at her sleeve.

'Come on,' he said in a low piping voice. 'We have to get going,' and he sounded like a spoiled child. She looked up at her husband still standing in the doorway. He was a big man, he completely filled that doorway, no light could get past him. She said:

'You must walk in his footprints. You have no choice.'

Something in his face stiffened when she uttered those words, but she did not see that, for the man in the suit was impatient and had let go of her arm and was already on his way down to the jetty, and she hurried after him, and then they vanished round the house and were out of sight.

He stood there in his stockinged feet, looking out at the yard. Through the silence he heard them get into the boat and the oars being put in the rowlocks and the muffled splash when they hit the water the first time and the rhythmic creak of iron on wood as his wife started to row with those strong arms he knew so well from countless embraces during the nights and years that lay behind him. Yet again she was on her way upriver to visit the man from Oslo who lived in the cabin there. Every time something was wrong she had to go there, every time something important was in the offing she had to go there, and now she had a trembling halfwit in the boat who was probably from the same town, and it was the middle of the day with a harsh light on the snow, and he threw a last glance over the yard and made a choice he would come to regret, and then he closed the door and went into the living room and sat down there. The twins were still playing in the kitchen, he could hear them plainly through the wall. To them everything was still the same.

II

Now

I SIT ON THE BENCH FOR A LONG TIME gazing out over the lake. Lyra is running about. I don't know what is happening. Something slides off me. The nausea has gone, my thoughts are clear. I feel weightless. It is like being saved. From shipwreck, from obsession, from evil spirits. An exorcist has been here and left, taking with him all the mess. I breathe freely. There is still a future. I think of music. Most likely I will buy a CD player.

I come up the slope from the bridge with Lyra at my heels and see Lars standing in my yard. He is holding a chainsaw in one hand, the other grips one of the birch branches. He rocks the tree, but as far as I can see it does not budge. Only the branch gives a little. The sun has more yellow now, with a sharper light in my face. Lars wears a peaked cap he has pulled well down over his eyes, and when he hears me coming he turns and almost has to lean his head backwards to look out from under the brim to meet my gaze. Poker and Lyra play tag around the house as well as they can with the birch blocking the yard, and then they rush together in a mock fight, growling and whining and rolling around on the grass behind the shed, having a good time.

Lars grins and shakes the branch again.

'Shall we deal with it?' he says.

'Yes, please,' I say, giving my most enthusiastic smile. And I mean it. It is a relief. It may well be that I like Lars.

I have not been quite sure, but it may well turn out that way. I would not be surprised.

'But then you'd best cut that branch,' I say, pointing to the one that has torn the gutter down and now presses against the door of the shed. 'Because my saw is in there.'

'We'll soon see to that,' he says, pulling out the choke on his saw, which is a Husqvarna and not a Jonsered, and that too is a relief in a comic sort of way, as if we were doing something we are not in fact allowed to do, but which is certainly really fun, and he pulls the cord once or twice and slams the choke back in and then gripping the cord firmly he lets the saw sink as he pulls and it starts up with a fine growl, and in a trice the branch is off and cut into four parts. The door is unblocked. It is an encouraging sight. I push the overhanging gutter aside and go in to fetch my saw, which is still on the bench where I left it, and take the yellow can of two-stroke petrol out with me. There is a little left. I put the saw down on the grass on its side and squat down to unscrew the petrol tank and pour, and it fills right up and then the can is empty. I do not spill any of it, my hand is steady, and that is a good thing when someone is watching.

'I have a couple of cans of petrol in my shed,' says Lars. 'So we can go on until we're finished. No sense in breaking off to drive into the village when there is a job to be done.'

'No sense at all,' I say and have no wish to do so; going into the village now. There is nothing I need from the shop, and this is not the day for social profligacy. I start the Jonsered, and luckily succeed at the first try, and we attack the birch, Lars and I, from two angles; a pair of slightly stiff men between sixty and seventy with earmuffs

on their heads against the deafening howl from the saws
when they eat into the wood, and we bend over them and
hold our arms well away from our bodies to make sure the
dangerous chain is an extension of our will and not the
other way around, and we deal with the branches first
and cut them off close to the trunk and saw them into
suitable lengths and cut away everything I cannot use for
firewood and gather all that into a heap I can put a match
to later and have a bonfire in the November darkness.

I like watching Lars work. I would not call him brisk,
but he is systematic and moves more elegantly up to the
birch trunk with the heavy saw in his grasp than he does
out on the road with Poker. His style infects my style, and
that is how it usually is for me; the movement first and
then the comprehension, for gradually I realise that the
way he bends and moves and sometimes twists around
and leans is a logical way of balancing against the supple
line between the body's weight and the tug of the chain as
it takes hold of the trunk, and all this to give the saw the
easiest access to its goal with the least possible danger to
the human body, exposed as it is; one moment strong and
unassailable, and then a crash, and suddenly ripped to
shreds like a doll can be, and then everything is gone and
ruined forever, and I do not know whether he thinks like
this, Lars, as he wields the chainsaw with such aplomb.
Probably he does not, but I do, several times over, cannot stop myself when it first comes to mind, and it does
not brighten my spirits. It's of no consequence though, I
am used to it, but I am sure his mother's mind was full of
thoughts like that when she rowed for her life upriver that
day in the late autumn of 1944, Lars rolling around on
the kitchen floor merrily mock-fighting his twin brother

Odd, not knowing what was going on around him, what
it could lead to, not knowing that three years later he
would shoot the life out of that very twin Odd with his
big brother Jon's gun and tear his body to shreds. No-one
could know that, and outside it was day still with a steel-
grey light on the snow-covered fields, and on the water
his mother tried to make it look like any of her numerous
trips up to the summer cabin.

I can picture it well.

Her blue mittens gripping the oars and her boots
braced against the bottom planks and her misty-white
breath coming out in hoarse gasps, and the stranger in
his summer shoes between her legs on the bottom of the
boat, his arms clutching the grey bag he would not let go
of, and he was no warmer now in his thin trousers. He
really was shaking violently, thumping on the woodwork
like a two-stroke motor of some yet undiscovered make;
she had never seen anything like it and was afraid that on
land they would hear this new engine of hers.

I can picture it well.

The German motorcycle with the sidecar calmly driving up the main road lately cleared of snow, and then
turning into the yard of precisely that farm, with no ap-
parent motive, no-one ever understood what the rider
was actually looking for. Maybe he was just lonely and
longing for a person to talk to, or wanting badly to smoke
a cigarette, and then finding his last match had been used
when he was about to light up and so came to borrow a
box of matches and have someone stand with him as he
smoked, looking at the landscape and the river, and there
was no-one else that he wanted to be just then than one
of two men from two different countries fraternising over

an innocent cigarette, distant from all evils of war, or else there was some other reason that no-one could guess at, either then or later. Whichever, he stopped the motor-bike in the yard, dismounted and walked unhurriedly towards the door of the farmhouse. But he never reached it. He suddenly came to a halt and stared at the ground, and then he started to walk back and forth, and then in a circle, and he squatted down, and finally he walked down past the house to the river and right onto the jetty. What happened to him there was that a light was lit in the huge darkness of his mind. The coin dropped into the machine in the right place, and a 'click' could be heard. Now everything was clear to him. And he was short of time. He ran back and threw himself onto his motorbike and immediately stamped hard on the start pedal, but damn it the motor would not start, and he tried again and again and then once more, and it suddenly came to life like a shot, and he bent over the handlebars and roared down the farm road and swerved onto the main road with the empty sidecar rattling on the outside in a spray of snow. Coming round that very bend was Jon, on his way home from school with his school bag under his arm, and he heard the motorcycle, and only just managed to throw himself into the ditch to avoid being run over and maybe injured for life. In the fall the buckle on his bag broke, and his books sailed out in all directions. But the soldier could not have cared less, he just gave it more throttle and vanished towards the crossroads where the shop and the church were, and the bridge crossed the river.

I can picture it well.

Jon in the ditch, picking books out of the snow while his mother is still on the river with the man in the suit flattening himself against the bottom of the boat. It is hard work rowing against the current with two people on board even though it is not so strong at this time of year, and they make slow progress. It is a good way up to the cabin yet where my father bends over a table in the out-house doing some carpentry, totally unaware that she is on her way. The man in the boat trembles and gabbles to himself, and then he weeps a little and gabbles again, and the woman at the oars pleads with him to be quiet, but he clutches the straps of his bag and is lost in his own world.

Franz stood in his kitchen with the window open, for he had stoked up his fire when he came home from working in the forest, and now it was so hot in the room that he had to let some air in. It was still daylight, and he stood there smoking and trying to work out why he had never married. It was something he brooded on every year at the time when the cold came creeping in, and he kept it up until Christmas and after, but at the beginning of the new year he threw it off. The lack of offers was not the reason, but when he stood there smoking by the open window, he just could not remember what the reason had been, and it seemed an absurd situation just then, to be living alone. And then he heard a motorcycle approach-ing up the road at great speed on the other side of the river. The bridge was fifty metres from his house, and a further twenty metres along on the opposite side stood the guard in his long grey-green overcoat with the sub-machine gun sticking up behind his shoulder, and he was cold and bored. He too heard the motorcycle, and he turned towards the rising volume of sound and took a few steps in that direction. Now Franz could just see the helmeted head of the rider appearing from behind a thicket over there, and then the whole motorcycle came into view with the rider bent over the handlebars to minimise the air resistance, and he had just a few hundred metres left before the crossroads. It had been misty and overcast all day, and now just before the sun was about to go down there it suddenly was in the southwest, throwing a golden light through the valley at a low slant, and it lit up the river and all that was on it and sent a dazzling ray into Franz's eyes and woke him from his thoughts about a possible marriage and the long line of blonde and dark-haired candidates he suspected would have queued up for him, and then it came to him what it was he was actually looking at up there on the road. He hurled his cigarette out the window, whipped round and ran out into the hallway, pulling a knife from his belt, and fell to his knees and rolled up the rag rug. There was a crack in the floorboards which he stuck the knife into hard and bent it upwards, and four boards that were fastened together tilted up, and he put them aside and put his hand into the space underneath. He had always known that this day would come. He was prepared. There was no time for hesitating, and not even for a moment did he hesitate. From the small space he brought out a detonator, quickly checked that the leads were in place and had not become tangled, and he placed it levelly between his knees, drew a deep breath as he took a firm hold of the handle, and then slammed it down. His house shook and the windows rattled, and he breathed out again and put the detonator back in its small space, laid the floorboards into the square opening and tapped them into place with his clenched fist and rolled the rag rug over the spot so that everything looked the way it had just a moment before. He rose to his feet and ran to look out the window. The bridge was shattered and parts of the wooden structure still whirled in the air in slow motion, on their way back down in the sudden silence after the explosion, and some of the planks hit the stones on the bank in a strangely soundless way and some fell in the water and started to drift with the current, and it seemed to Franz he saw it all through glass even though the window was open.

On the other side of the wrecked bridge the guard lay headlong in the snow with his nose to the ground a good way from the place where Franz had last seen him. The motorcycle had not made it in time, and now it slowed down and moved almost tentatively towards the body in the snow and stopped. The rider dismounted, took his helmet off and held it under his arm as if he was going to a funeral and walked the last metres to the guard and stood over him lowering his head. A gust of wind pulled at his hair. He was just a boy. He sank down to his knees beside what might well be his best friend, but then the guard pushed himself up on his hands and was not dead. He stayed in that position and could be seen to be vomiting, and then he got to his feet with his machine gun as a support and the motorcyclist too got to his feet and bent forward and said something to him, but the guard shook his head and pointed to his ears. He could not hear a thing. They both turned and looked at the bridge, which was no longer there, and then they ran to the motorcycle, and the guard got into the sidecar and the driver onto his seat, and he got the motor running again and turned out of the square. Not towards the farm where they were billeted with the rest of the patrol, but back down the road he had just ridden up, and he gave it as much throttle as he dared, and the machine had to work harder now with a passenger in the sidecar, but then it picked up speed, and when they passed Barkald's farm a few minutes later it was going really fast. Shortly afterwards they made a sharp turn off the road, and both leaned hard over as if in a sailing boat in a strong wind to make the turn without losing balance. The sidecar left the ground for a moment, and they roared out onto the snow-covered field and straight for the fence and the gate they did not bother to open but just drove right through with a crash that made the bars fly to all sides and hit their helmets, but they did not stop and there was only just enough room between the gateposts. And then they sped across the field close to the wire fence with the fence posts ticking past, and the machine bumping and swinging from side to side over the tussocks on its way down to the river along the path my father used to take when he was going to the shop to fetch 'the mail', and where I too used to go, only four years later, with my friend Jon who one day just disappeared out of my life because one of his brothers had shot the other out of his life with a gun that he, Jon, had forgotten to unload. It was high summer then, he was his brothers' keeper, and in one instant everything was changed and destroyed.

On the other side of the river Jon's mother had just landed her boat beside the one my father used, and jumped ashore to haul it far enough up for the current not to pull it back and then perhaps take it over to the other bank where it had better not be, and the man in the suit got up impatiently and stupidly tried to jump out before she had finished. It was no success. He fell forward as she jerked the bow and because he kept his hands tightly round the bag he fell and banged his head against a thwart. She was on the verge of tears then.

'Goddamn it, can't you do *anything* right?' the woman yelled, she who had hardly uttered a single swearword in her life, and though she knew it was a mistake to shout, she could not help it, and she took hold of his jacket and with a violent jerk hauled him like an unresisting sack out of the boat. As she straightened herself she both saw and heard the motorcycle roaring across the field on the opposite side, and my father came storming out of the shed beside the cabin, because he too had heard it and immediately realised something was wrong. He could see them at the end of the path by the water, Jon's mother in her cap and mittens and the stranger in his suit on all fours beside the boat, and the motorcycle, which had stopped just before the last slope covered with gravel and boulders on the edge of the bank.

'Get to your feet!' screamed Jon's mother into the suited man's ear, pulling at his jacket, and the boy in German uniform shouted:

'Halt!' as he rushed down the slope with the guard at his heels, and is it true he also called out an imploring 'please' in German? Franz said so, he was sure of it: *'Bitte, bitte,'* he had shouted, the young soldier. In any case, they stopped at the water's edge, not wanting to jump in. It was too cold, it was too deep, and if they swam across they would be helpless targets and would certainly reach the other bank much further down on account of the current, which was not particularly strong at that time of year yet strong enough. On the top of the slope behind them the motorcycle was chuntering away like an animal out of breath, and they pulled their machine guns from their shoulders, and my father shouted:

'Run like hell!' and started to rush off himself, *towards* the river through the trees no-one had sacrificed to the logging yet, and he zigzagged between them using the wide trunks for cover, and right then the soldiers on the other side began shooting. Warning shots first, above the heads of the two making their way all too slowly up from the boat, and they heard the bullets strike the tree trunks with a splintering force and an alien sound she would always remember, Jon's mother later said. Nothing had ever made her so terrified as that particular sound, it was as if the pine trees groaned, and then they shot for real, and immediately hit the suited man. His dark jacket was an obvious target against the white bank, and he dropped his bag, fell flat into the snow and said to himself so quietly that Jon's mother could barely hear the words:

'Aaah. I knew it.'

And then he started to slide, back down the slope towards the boat, past the crooked pine that leaned out over the river, and he did not stop until one of his summer shoes touched the water. They hit him again, and then he said nothing more.

My father had stopped just up the path, sheltered by a spruce. He called:

'Pick up his bag and run over here!' and Jon's mother grabbed the bag in her blue mitten and ran bent over, zigzagging upwards, and maybe it was because they had never killed anyone before that the two soldiers were suddenly no longer shooting so intensively, or because the runner was a woman. Now the shots they fired were only meant to frighten, and Jon's mother came running up the path unscathed and along with my father right up to the cabin. They rushed inside and picked out their most important things and the documents my father had hidden. Through the window they saw two cars cross the field at high speed from the road, and soldiers jumping out and running down to the river. My father stuffed everything they needed into the suited man's bag and wrapped a sheet around it. Then they climbed out the window at the back, and with my father's long white underwear over their clothes they fled, hand in hand, more or less, to Sweden.

The sun had moved on, the blue kitchen turned shadowy, and the coffee in my cup was cold.

'Why are you telling me these things when my father will not talk about them?' I said.

'Because he asked me to,' said Franz. 'When the opportunity arose. And it did, now.'

12
Now

WHILE LARS AND I HAVE BEEN BUSY with the birch it has gradually turned colder, the sun is gone and a wind is rising. A grey layer of cloud floats across the sky like a duvet, the last strip of blue is being pushed against the eastern ridge and eventually disappears. We take a break, straighten our stiff backs and try to look as if it does not hurt. I am not very successful, I have to support my spine with a hand to stay just about upright, and for a moment we both look away. Then Lars rolls a cigarette and lights up, he leans against the outhouse door and smokes peacefully. I recall how good it was to have a smoke after a spell of work, in the company of the partner you had toiled with, and for the first time in many years I miss it. Then I look at the heap of logs where just now a large part of the tree lay spread. Lars looks at it too.

'Not bad,' he says calmly, smiling. 'We're halfway there.'

Lyra and Poker are exhausted too. They lie panting side by side on the doorstep. The chainsaws have been turned off. Everything is quiet. And then it starts to snow. It's one o'clock in the afternoon. I look up at the sky.

'Shit,' I say aloud.

He follows my gaze. 'It won't settle, it's too early, the ground isn't cold enough,' he says.

'You're probably right,' I say, 'but it worries me all the same. I don't quite know why.'

'Are you fearful of being snowed in?'

'Yes,' I say, feeling my face flush. 'That too.'

'Then you should get someone to clear it for you. That's what I've done. Åslien, a farmer up the road here. He always shows up, no matter when, he has cleared for me for several years now. It doesn't take him long once he's out. It's only a matter of going up our road and then down again with the snow plough. Takes him a quarter of an hour at most.'

'Right,' I say, clearing my throat and then going on: 'He's the one, I called him yesterday from the kiosk by the Co-op. That was no problem, he said, 75 kroner a time. Is that what you pay him?'

'Yes,' Lars says. 'That's it. So then you're on the safe side. This winter will be alright. But all that up there,' he says almost ominously, leaning backwards and looking up at the sky. 'Let it come down.' He smiles with a reckless air.

'How about it, shall we go on?' he says.

His attitude is contagious, I do feel like going on. But it surprises me, too, and worries me that I should depend on someone else to give me the strength to take on such a simple and necessary job. It's not as if I didn't have the time. Something inside me is changing, *I* am changing, from someone I knew well and blindly relied on, called 'the boy with the golden trousers' by those who loved him, who came up with an endless supply of shining coins whenever he put his hand in his pocket, into someone much less familiar to me and who really has no idea what kind of rubbish he has in his pockets, and I wonder how long this change has been under way. Three years, perhaps.

'Yes, certainly,' I say. 'Let's do that.'

———

Afterwards I ask him in, I do have to after all he has done. It is snowing quite hard, but not really settling on the ground. Not yet anyway. We have stacked some awesome piles against the outhouse wall, beside the logs from the dead spruce, and the yard is swept clean apart from the huge root we have decided to pull away with chains and a car in the morning. The chains are down in Lars' garage. But it will do for today, we are worn out and pretty hungry and thirsty for coffee. Considering the kind of start my day has had, I wonder how bright it was to work so hard, but my body feels good, it really does, and I am tired in a pleasant way, apart from my back, and that feels no different than it would normally have done, and I could not very well have let Lars clear my yard on his own.

I measure coffee into the filter and pour cold water into the jug and switch on the percolator, and then I cut some bread and put it in a basket and get butter out and meat and cheese from the fridge onto plates and fill a small yellow jug with milk for the coffee and put everything on the table with glasses and knives for two.

Lars sits on the woodbox by the stove. He looks young in his stockinged feet, as in fact everyone does sitting like that with their feet barely reaching the floor. Unlike mine, his hair is dry because he has had his cap on, and he has not said anything since he came in, just gazed musingly at the floor, and neither have I said anything and have been happy with that, as I am not used to small talk any more, and then he says:

'Shall I light the fire?'

'Fine,' I say. 'Do.' For it *is* true it's getting cold in here, and at the same time I'm a bit surprised that he should take charge in my house and in that way have an opinion about how I do things, I would never have done that my-self, but he did ask first, so I guess it is alright. Lars slips off the woodbox, lifts the lid and picks out three pieces of firewood and a couple of pages of last week's *Dagbladet,* which I keep in the box for that purpose, and in no time he has the fire kindled, much faster than I usually manage; he has done this all his life, and then the percolator on the worktop starts to crackle and spit; good old coffee-maker I have had so long, and moments later I go over and pour the coffee into a Thermos. Holding it in my hand I stand there for a minute trying to think of the one I used to have coffee with every morning for many, many years, but she eludes me and I cannot see her face. Instead I look out the window at the cleared yard where nothing but small heaps of golden sawdust lie around the big root and the heavy snowflakes silently sail down and stay for a few seconds on the ground before mysteriously vanishing. If it goes on like that all through the night it will certainly settle by morning.

Did I have breakfast this morning? I do not remem-ber, it seems so long ago. All kinds of things have hap-pened since then. But I am certainly hungry now. I turn from the window to Lars, open my hand towards the table and say:

'Do tuck in, it's all yours.'

'Many thanks,' he says, having closed the woodbox, and we sit down, a little shy both of us, and start to eat.

We do not say anything for the first few minutes. The food tastes surprisingly good, and I have to go and look in the bread bin to see if the loaf I bought is different from the kind I usually get at the shop, but it's the same old thing. I sit down again and go on eating and I must say I do enjoy it. I try to slow down to make it last, and Lars too goes on eating with his eyes on his plate. That's fine with me, I have no need for conversation, but then he raises his head and says:

'Of course, I was supposed to take over the farm.'

'Which farm was that?' I ask, although there can be only one farm in question. But I was not quite with him in my thoughts, and I wonder whether that is how we get to be after living alone for a long time, that in the middle of a train of thought we start talking out loud, that the difference between talking and not talking is slowly wiped out, that the unending, inner conversation we carry on with ourselves merges with the one we have with the few people we still see, and when you live alone for too long the line which divides the one from the other becomes vague, and you do not notice when you cross that line. Is this how my future looks?

'The farm at home. In the village, of course.'

There must be a hundred thousand villages in Norway, we're in one of them now, but of course I know where he means.

'You've probably wondered why I live here and not up in the village where I come from?' he says.

In fact I have not, not in the way he means, but perhaps I ought to have done. What I *have* wondered is how we can end up in the same place after all these years. How such a thing is possible.

'Yes, you could say I have,' I say.

'It was mine to take over, I was the only one at home. Jon was at sea, Odd was dead, I had worked on that farm all my life, every single day, I had never gone away on holiday, as people do now. And my father never came back, he fell ill. No-one ever knew what was wrong with him. He broke his leg and he broke something in his shoulder and was taken to the Innbygda hospital, in 1948 that was, you remember that year, I was just a boy then. But he never came back. And then the years went by, Jon came home from the sea. I did not recognise him. It had been as if they no longer existed, any of them. I didn't think about them. And then one day Jon came walking up the road from the bus and in at the door and said he was ready to take over the farm. He was twenty-four years old. It was his right, he said. My mother made no objection, and she did not interfere and speak up for me, but I remember her expression then, how she did not look straight at me at all. That farm was the only work I had ever done and knew anything about. Jon was tired of the sea, he had seen it all, he said. That may have been so. He had sent a few postcards through the years, from Port Said and such places, Aden, Karachi, Madras, the sort of places you don't know a thing about or where in the world they are until you look them up in your school atlas. M/S *Tijuka* one of the boats was called, I remember the envelopes well, they had the name of the boat stamped on the front, and it was a name like none I had ever seen. Jon did not seem well, if you ask me. He was thin, with a slouch, he couldn't run a farm, I thought. He looked like a druggie, those you see on the streets of Oslo nowadays, he was nervous and tetchy. But there was nothing I could do. It was his right.'

And then Lars falls silent. It has been a long speech coming from him. He starts to eat again, he has not kept up with me, but he too enjoys the food. I give him some more coffee and offer him milk, and he takes the little yellow jug and helps himself to a few drops on the top of his coffee and stays silent while he finishes his meal, and when his plate is empty he asks if he can have a smoke indoors here, and I say:

'Yes, of course you can,' and he rolls a fag from his packet of Red Mix and lights up and takes a drag, and sits gazing at the glowing cigarette, so then I ask:

'Then what did you do?' Lars raises his eyes from the cigarette and puts it back in his mouth to take a deep drag, and while he slowly blows out he makes a grotesque grimace as if to hide himself behind a halfwitted mask, and it is so unexpected that I am taken by surprise and sit there peering, I have never seen him like this before. It's really a comical sight, like a circus clown who can make everyone weep a second after they have all died of laughter or like Chaplin in some frightful dilemma, or some other of the old stars of the silent movies, like the one who was always squinting, and he has a rubber face, Lars, but there is nothing there for me to laugh at. He compresses his mouth into a thin line and squeezes his eyes tightly together, then he twists his whole face forty-five degrees to the right and down past his ear, or at least that's what it looks like and the features I have barely become familiar with shrink into wrinkles, and he freezes it in that position for a while before opening his eyes and letting each part of his face fall back into place while the smoke goes on seeping out past his lips, and I do not have the slightest idea what kind of performance I have just witnessed. He breathes heavily in and out and his eyes are moist when he looks straight at me and says:

'I left. The day of my twentieth birthday. I haven't been home since. Not for five minutes.'

It grows silent in my kitchen, Lars is silent and I am silent, then I say:

'I'll be damned.'

'I haven't seen my mother since I was twenty,' he says.

'Is she still alive?' I say.

'I don't know,' says Lars. 'I never tried to find out.'

I look out the window. I don't know whether I want to know about this. I feel a huge fatigue settling over me, covering me, and pulling me down. I only ask because I feel I ought to, because it obviously is important to Lars to tell me these things, and of course in a way they do interest me, if he only knew, but then I do not know whether I really want to know about them. They take up too much room. It has become hard to concentrate, my meeting with Lars has thrown me off balance, has made my plan for being here seem obscure, almost unimportant when I do not put my mind to it, I have to admit that. My mood takes me up and down like in a lift, from attic to cellar in a couple of hours, and now my days have turned out differently from what I had imagined. The slightest thing goes wrong and I build it up into catastrophic dimensions. Not that the birch tree was a small thing, that is not what I mean, and not that it hasn't turned out well either, because in fact it has, with Lars' help, but I really wanted to be alone. To solve my problems alone, one at a time, with clear thinking and good tools, like my father probably did those times at the cabin, took on one task after another, assessing it and putting out the tools he needed in a calculated order starting at one end and working his way through to the other, thinking and using his hands and enjoying what he did, in the same way I want to enjoy what I do, to solve the daily challenges that may be tricky enough, but within clear limits, with beginnings and ends to them that I can foresee, and then be tired in the evening but not exhausted, and wake up all rested in the morning, brew my coffee and light the stove and look out at the light that comes pink over the forest towards the lake and get dressed and walk the paths with Lyra, and then get on with the tasks I have decided shall fill that day. That is what I want, and I know I can do it, that I have it in me, the ability to be alone, and there is nothing to be afraid of. I have seen so many things and been part of so much in my life although I will not go into details now, for I have been lucky too, I have been 'the boy with the golden trousers', but it would be nice finally to have some rest.

But then there is Lars, whom I probably cannot avoid liking, there is Lars; who gets up from the table and pulls his cap back and forth over his hair until it finds the right place, but outside there is twilight now and certainly no sunshine any longer, and he thanks me for the meal in an awkward, formal manner as if we had just finished Christmas dinner and he was the guest wishing he were ten miles away. He probably feels more at ease outdoors with an axe in his hands or a saw than here in my house, and that's fine by me, I can understand that. I would have felt the same way if I had been the guest in his home.

I go into the hall and open the door for Lars and follow him out onto the doorstep, and there Poker sits waiting. And when I say good night and thanks for the help, and he says, we made a good job of that birch, and we'll deal with the root tomorrow with the chains, the dog pushes between us and sits down and stares hard at his master and starts growling, but then Lars just turns his back without a glance down and walks straight past Poker and down the two steps and on across the yard and down the hill towards his cottage. Poker stands there, confused, his tongue hanging out and he looks up at me where I lean against the door waiting, not uttering a word of command to set him free, and then he suddenly lowers his head and slinks after Lars with an unwilling air and almost shuffling steps, and if I were him now I would mend my manners double quick.

There is a thin layer of snow in the yard. I did not notice when it began to settle, but the temperature has dropped, it is still snowing, and I cannot see it letting up. I go in and close the door behind me and turn off the outside light. Lars has forgotten his working gloves, they are lying where he put them down on the shoe rack, and I pick them up and open the door and am about to call after him, but there is no point, he can get them tomorrow, he won't be starting any work where gloves are needed.

Lars. Who says he did not think of his brother during the years Jon was at sea but remembers the towns and the harbours he visited and what was printed on the envelopes he sent home and the names of the ships he signed on with and signed off from, and who followed with his finger in the atlas the routes the ships took. Already thin and slouching, Jon stands on deck close to the bows of M/S *Tijuka* grasping the rail tightly, peering defiantly with narrowed eyes at the coast they are nearing. They come from Marseilles, and Lars' finger has followed the boat past Sicily and the tip of Italy's boot, and diagonally past the Greek islands, and southeast of Crete something new is in the air, with a different consistency from only a day ago, but Jon does not realise yet that this new element in the air is Africa. And then Lars goes with him on the way in to Port Said in the innermost Mediterranean where they will discharge and load up again before the voyage takes them slowly through the Suez Canal with the desert on both sides for long stretches and a strange yellow light from billions of glittering grains of sand in the shining sun, and then lengthways across the Red Sea first to Djibouti in blazing heat and then on to Aden on the other side of the narrow strait that divides one world from another, all the time in the wake of the young poet Rimbaud, who sailed here nearly seventy years earlier to be another person from the one he was before and put everything behind him like a desert diver on his way to oblivion and later death, and I know this because I have read about it in a book. But Lars does not know, sitting with his atlas in front of him on the kitchen table in the house by the river, and *Jon* does not know, but in Port Said he sees his first African palm under the low and violently blue sky. He sees the flat roofs of the town, and he sees bazaars and markets down every street and right out on the wharfs and alongside the quay where the M/S *Tijuka* is moored. There is nothing but bazaars in that town, and voices shouting in every language wanting to sell you something, wanting you to come down the gangway, you standing up there with your hands gripping the rail so tightly and eyes like narrow slits, you come down and buy something you just have to own if you know your own good, it will make your life so happy you won't even recognise it, and there is *special price for you today*, and it is deafening and bewildering, there are cymbals and kettledrums, and smells that almost make him faint;

a mixture of overripe vegetables and indefinable meat he had no idea existed in this world. And there are spices and herbs and something from a fire he can glimpse at the very end of the quay, and he does not know what they are burning there, but it has a sharp smell, and he will not leave the ship. He does his work on the cargo, and sets to with all his youthful strength, but he does not walk down the gangway. Not on his watch below or on any other watch, and when darkness abruptly falls he stays there on deck watching life go on at a more subdued tempo in a blend of electric and other lights, and it all seems more alluring now than in the garish light of day, but more sinister too, with its flickering shadows and narrow alleyways. He is fifteen years old and he does not leave the ship in Port Said, nor in Aden nor Djibouti.

Jon

I wake in the night and sit up in bed to look into the darkness outside the window. It is still snowing, there is a high wind whirling out there, hurling snowflakes against the panes. Where the road leads down towards the river there is nothing but a huge white blanket without contours of any kind. I crawl out of bed, go into the kitchen and light the small lamp above the cooker. Lyra raises her head from where she lies in her place by the black stove, but there is nothing wrong with her inner clock, she knows we are not going out now, it's only two in the morning. I go into the bathroom, or actually the cubbyhole off the hall, where I keep a wash-bowl, a pitcher of water and a bucket on the floor for when the weather is so bad I do not feel like going out behind the house. I pay a call there, then put on a sweater and a pair of socks and sit down at the kitchen table with a very modest dram and the final pages of *A Tale of Two Cities*. Sydney Carton's life is coming to an end, blood running all about him, through a red veil he sees the guillotine working rhythmically; heads falling into the basket until it is full and then is replaced, and the women knitting in the stalls are counting: nineteen, twenty, twenty-one, twenty-two, and he kisses the woman standing in front of him in the queue and says farewell until we meet in a land where no time exists and no sorrow as in this, and soon he is the only one left, and he says to himself and the world: 'It is a far, far better thing that I do, than I have ever done . . .' It is not easy to disagree with him in such a situation. Poor Sydney Carton. Really entertaining reading, I must say. I smile to myself and take the book into the living room with me and put it in the bookshelf in its place among the other books by Dickens, and back in the kitchen I down the little dram in one swallow and turn off the light above the stove and go into the bedroom and lie down. I am asleep before my head hits the pillow.

At five o'clock I am woken by the drone of a tractor and the scraping, rattling sound of a snowplough on its way up the road towards my house. I see its lights through the window and realise at once what it is and just turn over and fall asleep again, without having the time to think one single sceptical thought.

13

In between
Back in time
after the
timber
Cutting

AFTER MY MORNING WITH FRANZ the valley looked different. The forest was different, and the fields were, and maybe the river was the same, yet somehow altered, and that, too, was how my father seemed to me when I thought of the stories Franz had told me about him and just as much after what I had seen him do on the jetty in front of Jon's house. I did not know whether he was more distant now or maybe closer to me, whether he was easier to understand or harder, but he was certainly different, and I could not talk to him about it, for *he* was not the one who had opened that door, and so I had no right to enter in, and I did not even know if I wanted to.

Now I could see how he was impatient. Not that he was brusque or short-fused in any manner, he was just the way he had been since we arrived on the bus, and though it was true I felt a great difference inside myself thinking of him, I could not *see* any difference. But now he was tired of waiting. He wanted the timber on its way. Regardless of what we had been doing during the day, gone to the shop, or rowed upriver to the rapids by the bridge to fish from the boat on the way back down, or worked on carpentry in the yard or walked around in the felling waste wearing gloves and clearing up the tangled chaos and hauling branches onto a bonfire we could light up later when the weather would allow, he did not want to leave a mess behind him when the future time arrived, he had to go down to the two piles of timber by the river at least twice every evening to push at them and thump the timber and calculate the angle and the distance to the water to see whether the trunks would land correctly when they took off and then go through it all once more. This was actually quite unnecessary, if you asked me, for everyone could see that the trunks would slide straight into the river and would not get hooked up in any obstacle on the way down, and he probably knew that too. But he could not keep away. Sometimes he stood there a long time just sniffing the wood, even pressing his nose against the bare timber where the bark had been stripped off and the resin was shining still, and breathing it deeply in, and I did not know if he did that because it was something he liked to do, which I did, or whether his nose could read some information from inside it to which we other mortals had no access. If so, whether this information was good or bad I had no way of knowing, but it did not make his impatience any weaker. Then it rained heavily for two days, and the next evening he went up the road to Franz to talk to him, and he stayed there a long time. When he came back I was in the top bunk reading by the light of a small paraffin lamp, for the evenings were darker now, and he came into the room and leaned against my bed and said: 'We're going to take a chance on it tomorrow. We're sending the timber downriver.'

I could tell at once from my father's voice that Franz had not shared his view. I placed the bookmark in my book and leaned over the edge, and with my arms dangling I dropped the book onto the chair beside the bed and said:

'Good. I'm looking forward to it.' And that was true, I was. I looked forward to the physical side of it, to the pressure on my arms, to the trunks resisting me and then feeling them give way at last.

'That's good,' said my father. 'Franz will come down to help us. You'd better go to sleep and build up your energy for tomorrow. It won't be child's play, that's for sure, for there will only be the three of us, and there's a lot of timber. Now I'll just have a quick walk down there to do a bit of thinking. I'll be back in an hour.'

'That's alright,' I said.

He was going to the river to sit on a rock and gaze in front of him, and I was used to that, so I did not doubt he was telling the truth, for he often went to that rock.

'Shall I put the light out?' he said, and I said yes please, and he bent down and put his hand behind the top of the lamp and blew into the glass pipe so the flame went out and turned into a small red strip along the wick, and then that too was gone and it was dark, but not completely dark. I could see the grey edge of the forest outside the window and the grey sky above, and my father said 'Good night, Trond, see you tomorrow,' and I too said 'Good night and see you tomorrow,' and then he went out, and I turned towards the wall. Before I fell asleep I put my forehead against the coarse timbered wall sniffing the faint scent of forest it still held.

I was up once that night. I climbed cautiously down from the bunk and looked neither to the right nor left so as not to miss the door, and then I made a visit out behind the cabin. I stood there barelegged in only my pants with the wind in the trees high above me and the leaden clouds which I imagined were full of rain and soon would burst, but then I closed my eyes and lifted my face to the sky, and there was nothing coming down that I could feel. Only cool air on my skin and the scent of resin and timber, and the scent of earth, and a bird whose name I did not know hopping around in a thicket rustling and crackling and sending out a steady stream of thin piping sounds from the dense foliage a few paces from my foot. It was a strange, lonely sound out there in the night, but I did not know whether it was the bird I thought was lonely or if it was me.

When I went back inside my father was in bed sleeping as he had said he would be. I stayed there in the semi-darkness looking at his head on the pillow: his dark hair, the short beard, the closed eyes and his face far off in a dream somewhere that was not in this cabin with me. There was no way I could reach him now. His breathing sounded peaceful and content, as if he did not have a care in the world, and perhaps he did not, and neither should I have, but I was uneasy and didn't know what to think about anything at all, and if breathing was easy for him, for me it was not. I opened my mouth wide and sucked the air in hard three or four times before my chest opened up, and I must have been a weird sight panting away in that half-dark room, and then I climbed up past my father and pulled the duvet round me. I did not fall asleep at once but lay staring at the ceiling, studying the patterns I could just about glimpse and all the knot holes that seemed to be moving back and forth like tiny creatures with invisible legs, and I was stiff all over at first and then more relaxed as the minutes passed, or maybe it was hours. It was difficult to say, for I had no sense of time passing or the room I was in, everything just moved slowly around like the spokes of a huge wheel to which

I was strapped, with my neck to the hub and my feet to the outer rim of the circle. It made me dizzy and I opened my eyes wide so as not to be sick.

The next time I woke up it was already morning with light flooding the window-sill, and I had slept too long and felt tired and weary and had no urge to get up at all.

The door to the living room was open, as was the outside door, and if I propped myself up on my elbow I could see the sunshine slanting in on the glossy scrubbed floor. There was a smell of breakfast in the cabin and I heard my father and Franz talking in the yard. There was a calm, subdued, almost lazy note in between their words, and if the day before they had had a disagreement, they certainly had none now, but may have reached an understanding as to how important this logging job was to my father, and so they were taking their chances and had agreed that this was what they were good at, taking chances, though to me it seemed perfectly feasible to let the timber wait for a month or two or even until spring. Anyway, there they were in the yard standing in the sunshine and unhurriedly laying out a plan, so I could tell, for what they wanted to accomplish together that day, as they may have done so many times before when I knew nothing about it.

I lay back on the pillow and tried to think out what it was that made me feel so heavy and so weary, but nothing came to mind; no words, no images, merely a mauve tinge behind my eyelids and a dry sore feeling in my throat, and then I thought of the piled-up timber beside the river that would be going off any moment now, and I wanted to be part of that. I wanted to see the avalanche of logs hit the water, and watch the river bank emptying, and the smell of food from the kitchen alcove gave my stomach a sudden hollow feel, and I called through the door:

'Have you had breakfast?'

The two of them out there started laughing, and it was Franz who said:

'No, we're just hanging about here waiting for you.'

'Poor old men,' I called back. 'I'll be with you in a sec if there's food to be had,' and I decided that I was actually in fine fettle after all, and light as a feather. I pulled myself together in a flash and jumped out of bed as I usually did, with my hands gripping the side of the bunk, taking off by the bum, my legs swinging right from the top down to the floor in a telemark landing. But this time my thighs went on strike and my calves took the impact, and my right knee hit the floorboards and I fell over on my side. My knee hurt so badly I almost cried out. The two men outside must have heard the sound, for my father called:

'You alright in there?' but luckily he stayed where he was with Franz. I squeezed my eyes tight and called:

'Oh sure, everything's fine in here,' although that was not how it felt. I managed to get up on the chair by the bed and sat there with both hands round my knee. It did not feel as if anything was broken when I touched it, but the pain was almost unbearable and made me slightly desperate and dizzy and somewhat confused, and getting into my trousers was difficult, because I had to keep my right leg stiff, and I was on the point of giving up and climbing back into bed, if such a move had been possible.

But I got my trousers on at last, and then the rest of my clothes, and limped out into the living room and sat down with my leg straight out under the table before my father and Franz were done talking and came inside.

When we had finished our late breakfast the two men started washing up at once, because my father wanted to have a clean slate when he came home tired, he said, and not walk straight into slop and mess, and I did not know why but they just let me sit there although it was normally my duty to help with the dishes when my sister had not come with us from Oslo. In any case, I had nothing against being left alone.

They stood with their backs to the table, chatting and fooling around and clattering the cups and glasses, and Franz piped up with a song he had learned from his father about the wolverine that hung from the top of a tree. As it turned out my father knew that song too and had learned it from *his* father, and they bellowed it out in unison waving their dishcloths and washing-up brushes to the beat, and I *saw* that wolverine dangling helplessly from the top of a spruce, and my head felt so heavy and hard to hold up I seized the opportunity to rest it in my hands on the table in front of me, and sitting like that I may have dropped off for a few moments. But when my father said:

'Now we really can't mess about here any longer, we must get going, isn't that so, Trond?' I heard him clearly and replied with my mouth full of saliva:

'Yes, that's it,' and I lifted my head and wiped my mouth, and suddenly I did not feel too bad after all.

I walked behind them across the yard to the shed,

trying to limp as little as possible, and from among the tools I picked up a pike pole and hung a coil of rope over my shoulder, and my father took a pike pole too and two axes and a sheath knife, and Franz took a crowbar and a freshly sharpened saw, and all this we kept in the shed and more too: saws and hammers and two scythes and clamps and two planes and chisels of different sizes, and various files hung from nails in rows along the wall, and there were angle-irons and a good many tools whose use I did not know, for it was a well-equipped workshop my father had in that shed, and he loved those tools and sharpened them and polished them and soaked them with different oils so they would smell good and keep for a long time, and each and every thing had its appointed place where it hung or stood and was always ready for use.

My father closed the shed door and put the peg in place, and then the three of us walked in line carrying the tools under our arms and on our shoulders along the path to the river and the two piles of timber with my father first and me at the rear. And the sun was shining and flashing in the river, which was running high after several days of rain, and it would have been a perfect picture of that summer and the things we were doing together, if I were not still hobbling badly on one leg, and because inside me, not far from where my soul was, as I saw it, there was something worn and tired that just now had made my ankles and thighs too weak to carry the weight they normally would have done.

When we arrived at the river bank we put our tools down on the stones, and my father and Franz walked around the first pile and stopped side by side with their backs to the sparkling, swollen river, and with their heads cocked and their hands on their hips they studied the heavy timber stacked up against two strong, vertical bars. The bars were held in place by slanting logs securely set into the ground, and the idea was that when the slanting logs were removed the bars would fall straight down, and the pile of timber slide with a rush and all the logs roll forward over the bars lying like rails and on down into the water if the distance and incline were correct. And according to my father and Franz, everything was correct. What they did next was to kneel down and dig away the gravel and stones from around the ends of the slanting logs to make them easier to pull away. When that was done, they picked up their ropes and they each fastened theirs round a log and backed well out to the sides of the pile with the rope end in their hand as they did not want to get in the way of the moving timber. There were many ways of doing this, and this variant was Franz's patent. He had never managed to get all the timber out into the water in one slip, he said, and nor did he think he would succeed this time for there had to be a very special slope for that, and accordingly a really substantial weight, and it took bars and stays as strong as hell to do it and a lot of luck too, and then it all would be pretty risky. But of course, if you want a life of leisure, you have to take a big risk once in a while, according to Franz.

Now they tightened the rope from each end and dug their heels firmly into the ground, and then they counted aloud in chorus: Five, four, three, two, one, now! And they pulled with all their strength so the ropes crackled and the veins stood out on their foreheads and their faces darkened. Not a thing happened. The bars stayed where they were. Franz counted down once more and shouted: Now! And they pulled again and groaned in rhythm, and nothing moved except the features of the two men, who ground their teeth and narrowed their eyes to slits. But whatever the grimaces they made, it did not help, nor when they pulled with their uttermost strength. The bars stood firm.

'Shit,' my father said.

'Flaming hell,' said Franz.

'We'll have to cut them with the axe,' my father said.

'That's risky,' Franz said. 'We could get the whole slagheap on our heads.'

'I know,' my father said. And then they went and picked up their axes from the stack of tools and went back to the front of the timber pile and laid into the slanting stays with arms and bodies almost bursting with irritation at not succeeding with their plan at the first try, for they were spoiled in that way, and Franz shouted 'Flaming hell' again, and then he said:

'Let's chop in time.'

'So we will,' my father said, and they changed rhythm and synchronised their strokes, and the sound of the axe blows was like one sharp crack each time. I could see they liked doing this, for Franz suddenly smiled and laughed, and my father smiled, and I wished I were like them, that I had a friend like Franz I could swing my axe with and make plans and use my strength with and laugh and cut logs with by a river like this one, which was always the same and yet was new, as now, but the only possible friend had disappeared and no-one talked about him any more. Of course I had my father, but it was not the same. He was a grown man with a secret life behind the one that I knew about, and maybe even one behind that, and I no longer knew if I could trust him.

Now he went faster with the axe while Franz followed suit, and then my father too began to laugh and swung his axe with added strength, and then I heard a creak from where the axe struck. He yelled: 'Run like hell!' and turned on his heel and threw himself out to the side. Franz laughed aloud and did the same. The stays broke almost simultaneously. They overlapped and the bars fell forwards perfectly according to plan, and then the pile began to slide with the sound of a hundred heavy bells that positively sang out across the water and into the forest, and at least half the trunks went tumbling off and almost leaped into the river. The spray boiled up, there was an impressive chaos of logs and water, and I was glad I was there to see it.

But there was still a lot of timber left, and it all had to go. The three of us set to work with our pike poles, and we hauled and pushed and pulled, and sometimes we used the crowbar to pry the logs apart when they were stuck fast, and sometimes the rope to pull them free when they were tangled up, and one by one they gave way. We rolled them, two of us at a time, with the pike poles out into the river, and then there was a splash, and they suddenly drifted off with dignified calm on the current down through the valley, on their way to Sweden.

I soon felt myself getting tired. The special feeling I was waiting for that would lift me and intoxicate me and give me that extra strength for the work, and swing me so easily from grip to grip, never took hold of the muscles in my legs or my arms or anywhere else as I had hoped for. Instead I felt heavy and drained and had to concentrate carefully on doing one thing then the next to prevent the others from seeing the state I was in. My knee hurt, and I was relieved when my father finally called out that it was time for a break. Most of the timber had been launched, only a few small trunks were left, but we had one more pile to send off. I crept over to the pine tree with the wooden cross on its trunk that Franz had put up one winter night in 1944 because a man from Oslo wearing far too thin and baggy trousers had been killed there, by German bullets, and I lay down in the heather under the cross, resting my head on one of the big roots, and fell asleep at once.

When I woke up, Jon's mother was kneeling over me with the sun behind her head and a hand in my hair, and she had the blue cotton dress on with the yellow flowers and a serious look on her face, and she asked me if I was hungry. For a second there I was the man with the baggy trousers, who was not dead after all, but who had come to himself and looked up at her still standing at his side, but then he slipped away and vanished. I blinked and felt myself blush and immediately realised that it was because I had been dreaming about her, and I did not remember what, but there had been an intense and strange warmth in the dream I could not admit to now with her eyes in mine. I nodded my head and trying to smile I began to push myself up on one arm.

'I'm coming,' I said, and she said:

'Fine, come along then, food's ready now,' and she smiled so unexpectedly I had to look away, look out across the water that was swelling by behind her back to the

other bank where suddenly two of Barkald's horses were
standing by the fence at the top of the field staring over
at us with their ears pricked and hooves stamping, like
two ghost horses sent here to warn of disasters to come.

She rose from her knees to her feet in one gliding
movement as if it was the easiest thing in the world to do
and went over to the crackling fire my father or Franz had
made in the empty space where the first pile had been.
There was a smell of roasting meat and coffee in the air,
and the smell of smoke, and timber and heather and sun-
warmed stones and some special scent I had not noticed
anywhere else than by this river, and I did not know what
it was made of if not a combination of all that was there; a
common denominator, a sum, and if I left and did not return I would never be able to experience it again.

Not far from the fire, Lars sat on a rock beside the water.
In his hand he had a bundle of coarse twigs, and he broke
them into equal lengths and stacked them in a pile right
down by the river on a grassy slope beside the rock, and at
the front of the pile he had fixed two sharp twigs for bars.
He laid all the twigs up against them. It looked really good
in miniature, like a proper pile of logs. I went over to him
and squatted down. My leg felt much better now after the
rest, so maybe I would not be crippled after all. I said:

'That pile looks really great.'

'It's just a few twigs,' he said, and his voice was low
and serious, and he did not turn round.

'We-e-ll,' I said, 'maybe it is. But it's great all the same.
Like the real thing, only in miniature.'

'I don't know what minnyture means,' said Lars
softly.

I searched my mind. I didn't really know either, but I said:

'It's when something that's very tiny looks just the same as something that's big. It's just little, that's all. Do you understand?'

'Tsk. It's only a few twigs.'

'OK, fine,' I said. 'It's only a few twigs. Aren't you going to have some lunch?'

He shook his head. 'No,' he said, almost inaudibly. 'I'm not going to have any lunch.' He said 'have lunch' as I said it, and not just 'eat' as he would otherwise have done.

'Oh, well,' I said. 'That's fine, too. Suit yourself?' Carefully I stood up, my weight on my left leg.

'Well, *I'm* hungry,' I said, turning away and taking a step or two, and then I heard him say:

'I shot my brother, I did.'

I turned and retraced the two steps. My mouth went dry. I almost whispered:

'I know. But it wasn't your fault. You didn't know the gun was loaded.'

'No,' he said. 'I didn't know that.'

'It was an accident.'

'Yes. It was an accident.'

'Are you sure you don't want something to eat?'

'Yes,' he said. 'I'll stay here.'

'That's alright,' I said. 'You can come along later when you feel hungry,' and I looked at his hair and the little I could see of his face, he was only ten, for God's sake, and nothing moved, and he had no more to say.

I walked up to the bonfire where my father sat quite

relaxed with his back to the river next to Jon's mother on one of the logs that was still lying there. They were not tight together as they had been on the jetty that morning, but still quite close, and those backs seemed so much at ease and almost smug, and they suddenly made me feel intensely irritated. Franz sat on his own on a tree stump opposite them with a tin plate in his hand, I saw his bearded face through the fire and the transparent smoke, and they had already started eating.

'Come here, Trond, and sit down,' said Franz, a bit awkwardly, patting a stump near his one. 'You need food now. There's a lot more work to do. To survive we'll have to eat.'

But I did not sit down on that stump. I did something I thought was unheard of then, and I still do, because I shoved my way up behind my father and Jon's mother and flung one leg over the log they sat on and pushed myself right between them. There really was not room enough so I pushed hard against the both of them and against her in particular and my aggressive movements were sharp against her softness, and it made me feel sad doing it, but I did it just the same, and she pulled away, and my father sat stiff as a board. I said:

'Now this is a great place to sit.'

'You think so, do you?' my father said.

'Sure,' I said. 'In such good company.' I looked straight into Franz's eyes and kept my gaze there, and his eyes started to shift and then, hardly chewing at all, he fixed them on his plate, making a peculiar face. I took a plate for myself and a fork, and I leaned forward to help myself from the frying pan that was nicely arranged on a rock at the fire's edge.

'This looks really tasty,' I said, laughing, and I could hear my voice having a shrill tone to it and coming out much louder than I had meant.

14

Now

I FLOUNDER MY WAY UP FROM THE DREAM towards the light, and I do see the light above me. It's like being under water; the glimmering blue surface up there, so close and yet so out of reach, for nothing moves swiftly in the lilac-coloured levels down here, and I have been in this place before, but now I do not know whether I can get up in time. I stretch my arms as far as I can, dizzy with exhaustion, and suddenly feel the cold air on my palms, and I use my legs to make speed upwards and my face breaks through the topmost gauzy layer and I open my mouth for air. Then I open my eyes and it is not light after all, but just as dark as in the depths. The disappointment tastes like ash in my mouth, this is not where I want to be. I take a deep breath and close my lips tight and am about to dive back when I realise it's my bed I am in, under the duvet, in this room beside the kitchen, it is early morning and still pitch dark, and I do not need to hold my breath any longer. I let it go and laugh in relief into the pillow, and then I start to weep before I'm able to understand why. That is something new, I cannot remember the last time I wept, and I do weep for a short while, and then it strikes me: if one morning I do not reach that surface, does that mean I am dying?

But that is not why I am weeping. I could have gone outside and laid myself down in the snow until the cold made me numb, to get as close to death as possible, to find out what it feels like. I could easily have made myself

ready. But then it is not death I fear. I turn to the small
bedside table and look at the shining face of the clock.
It says six. It's my time. I have to get going. I sweep the
duvet aside and swing myself up. This time my back feels
fine, and I sit on the edge of the bed with my feet on a
rug I have put on the floor so that the shock to my soles
will not be so terrible in the cold season. I ought to lay a
new floor with insulation. Maybe in the spring I will, if
I'm not skint. Of course I won't be skint. When will I stop
worrying about that? I switch on the bedside light. I feel
for my trousers hanging over a chair and get my hands on
them and take hold, but then I stop there. I don't know. I
am not ready, it seems. There are things I must do. There
are floorboards to replace on the doorstep before someone falls through and breaks a leg, that was what I was
going to do today. I have bought impregnated boards and
three-inch nails, that should do it, four-inch ones would
be too long, I think, and then there's the splitting of the
chunks from the fallen spruce into firewood sizes, that remains to be done still and it goes without saying should
not be postponed now that winter is coming in earnest.
That's how it looks, anyway, and then Lars is coming up
later, and we will haul the big root off with chains and a
car. It will be good fun, I reckon, to deal with that. I look
out the window. It has stopped snowing. I can faintly see
the outlines of the piled-up snowbank down the road.
Perhaps working outdoors will not be so easy today.

I let go of my trousers and lie down again. There was
something about that dream which was disturbing. I
know I can work it out if I try, I'm good at that, I used to
be anyway, but I don't know whether I want to. It was an
erotic dream, I often have them, I admit it, after all they

are not reserved for teenagers. Jon's mother was in it, as she was that summer of 1948, and I as I am now, sixty-seven years old and more than fifty years later, and maybe my father was in it somewhere, in the background, in the shadows, it seems he was, and if I so much as touch the dream there is a tension in my gut. I think I must let it go, let it fall back and sink down to rest among the others I have had and do not dare to touch. That part of my life when I could turn the dreams to some use is behind me now. I am not going to change anything any more. I am staying here. If I can manage. That is my plan.

So I get up. Six fifteen. Lyra leaves her place beside the stove and goes to the kitchen door to wait. She turns her head and looks at me, and there is a trustfulness in that look I probably do not deserve. But maybe that is not the point, to deserve it or not, perhaps it just exists, that trust, disconnected from who you are and what you have done, and is not to be measured in any way. That's a nice thought. Good dog, Lyra, I think, good dog. I open the door and let her out into the hall and then onto the door-step. I switch on the outside light from inside and follow her out and stand there, looking. Lyra jumps straight out into the yellow-lit snow lying in huge drifts except where Åslien has shovelled the yard so expertly in a big circle and avoided my car by a few centimetres only and pushed the big root back and forth with the ploughshare as it must have been in the way the whole time, and finally moved it to the side of the yard settled where it is now; ready and accessible for later removal. He has even cleared a strip alongside one wall of the house where I usually go for a leak at the edge of the wood when I don't want to over-use the outdoor lavatory. Maybe he was suggesting

I should leave my car there in the future so it will not be in the tractor's way, or perhaps he has an outdoor lavatory himself?

I leave Lyra in the yard to sniff around on her own in the new white world and close the door and go in to make a fire in the stove. No problem with that today, soon it is crackling away with a crisp and reassuring sound behind the black iron plates, and I don't switch on the ceiling light at once but leave the room in twilight so the yellow flames in the stove flicker brightly over the floor and walls. The sight of them slows my breathing down and makes me calm as it must have done for men through thousands of years: let the wolves howl, here by the fire it's safe.

I lay the table for breakfast still without the light on. Then I let Lyra in from the cold so she can lie beside the stove a while before we go out together. I sit down and look out the window. I have turned the outside light off again so only the surface of things themselves will shine, but it is too early still for daylight to come, only the faintest tinge of pink above the trees towards the lake; vague streaks like the marks of a hard crayon, and nevertheless everything stands out more distinctly than before, because of the snow; a clear line between sky and earth, and *that* is something new this autumn. And then I eat slowly, not thinking of the dream any more, and when I have finished I clear the table and go out into the hall and put my tall boots on and the warm old pea jacket and a cap with earflaps and mittens and the woollen scarf I have worn round my neck for at least twenty years, which someone knitted for me when I was a single and divorced man, and now I cannot recall her name, but I remember her hands from the time we spent together; they were never still. Apart from that she was still and discreet in her ways; only the click of her knitting needles could be heard through the silence, and it was all too low-key for me, and the relationship dwindled quietly into nothing.

Lyra wags her tail at the door, alert and ready, and I take the torch from its shelf and unscrew one end and exchange the old batteries for the new ones waiting on that same shelf, and then we're off. I go first and she follows when she is told. I am the boss, we both know that, but she is happy to wait because she knows our system too and smiles as only a dog can smile and jumps a good metre into the air straight up and out over the whole flight of steps when I quietly say: Come on! She lands almost in my arms, standing. She still has the puppy inside her.

I switch on the torch and we start walking down the slope where Åslien has cleared the snow into sharply edged banks in an elegant curve over to the bridge across the little river and Lars' cottage on the other side and pretty certainly on to the highway right through the spruce trees, and then we stop and I point the torch at the path we usually take along the stream to the lake. There is a lot of snow there now and I don't know whether I can cope with trudging that way. But then there is only one other direction I can choose, and that is straight ahead. We have never before been that way together, the last stretch to the main road and then along it, because it means I have to put Lyra on the lead on account of the traffic, and it is not very satisfying for either of us. In that case I might as well have stayed on in the city, plodding up and down the same dreary streets I had walked for three years thinking there must be an end to this, now something will have to happen, or I am finished. So I say to myself: why should I not get tired, what else is there in my life I am saving my strength for? And I stride over the snowbank and the first drifts and start to walk with my torch on, and in some places the path has been blown clear of snow and feels nice and hard to walk on, while in others the snow lies in high drifts, and it was really smart to put my tall boots on, I lift them well and swing one leg before the other in front of me, the right leg first and let it sink, and then the left one and let it sink, and then the same movement over again, and in that way I am toiling through the worst places. The sky above me is clearing and some stars can be seen, rather pale now at night's end, but there will be no more snow for now. When it is fully light the sun will come out, if not as blazing or as vibrantly hot as a day it suddenly occurs to me to think back on now, one day in late June 1945, when my sister and I stood at the window on the first floor with a view over the inner Oslo fjord and of Nesoddlandet and the Bunnefjord, and it was summertime with a dazzling light on the water and hysterical boats zigzagging from shore to shore, cruising on with all sails set in the brilliance of liberated Norway and they almost tacked with enthusiasm and never grew tired, and they sang, those who were on board, and were not ashamed, and that of course was fine for them. But I was tired of it all already, worn out with waiting, I had seen those people so many times, on Karl Johan Street in town and on Østmarksetra in the woods, at Ingierstrand baths and at Fagerstrand when we went out there in a borrowed boat and many other places where they hollered and yelled and never realised the party was over. That was why we were not gazing out to the fjord that

Father returns from War

day, nothing came from that direction worth waiting
for. What we did, my sister and I, was to peer down
the road where my father came slowly walking up the
steep Nielsenbakken from Ljan Station on his way home
from Sweden after the war, much delayed, with much
caution, in a worn grey suit and a grey sack on his back
from which something poked up that looked like a fishing rod, and he did not drag his foot, he had no limp,
he was not wounded that we could see, but still he came
so slowly up, as if inside a vast silence, inside a vacuum,
and why we stood there at the window and had not been
to the station well before the train arrived or down in the
road to meet him and greet him, I cannot today remember.
Perhaps we were shy. I know at least I must have been, as
I always was shy, and my mother stood in the open doorway on the ground floor biting her lip and twisting the
soaking handkerchief in her hand, unable to control her
feet. She was hopping up and down as if she had to go
to the bathroom, and then she could not hold herself
back any longer and pulled herself free of the door-frame
and ran down the road, and witnessed by spectators in
several gardens she threw herself at my father. That was
what she was supposed to do, of course, what she had to
do, and she was still young then and light on her feet,
but the way I remember her is the way she became later.
Bitter, marked and much heavier.

My father must have expected a reception like that,
I am convinced he did. We had not seen him for eight
months and had not heard a word until two days before, so we knew he was coming. My sister ran clattering
down the stairs and out into the road where she copied
every single movement my mother made, much to my

embarrassment, and I slowly followed; it was not easy for me to let myself get carried away, that was not who I was. I stopped by the letter box and leaned against it and looked at the two of them standing in the middle of the road clinging to my father. I glimpsed his face over their shoulders; confused at first and helpless, and then his eyes sought mine, and mine sought his. I nodded lightly. He nodded back and smiled faintly, a smile meant for me alone, a secret smile, and I realised that from now on it was all about the two of us, that we had a pact. And no matter how long he had been away he seemed closer that day than before the war started. I was twelve years old, and in the passing of one moment my life shifted from one point to another, from her to him, and took a new course.

But maybe I was too eager.

I puff my way right to the bench covered in snow at the edge of the water, or Swan Lake, as I name it now to myself, as a child would have done, and Swan Lake lies open and black in the torchlight. The ice has not settled yet, it has not been that cold. No swans to be seen either, at this time. Probably they stay in the dense rushes on dry land through the night, with their long necks like feather-clad loops in white bows, and their heads under their wings, I can picture it well, and they do not swim out until light has come to graze along the bank while the water is still open. What they will do when the ice settles is something I have not thought about, why do they not fly south to ice-free lakes, will they stay here until spring? Do swans stay in Norway during wintertime? I must find that out.

Using my arm I shovel snow off the bench, making big circular movements and then with my mittens brush off what is still there and I pull my jacket well down over my behind and sit down. Lyra snorts at the snow and romps about happily, in one spot she throws herself down and rolls over again and again, her legs in the air, twisting and turning her back in the snow with delight at absorbing into her fur the scent of something that has been here before. A fox maybe. If so she will have to be washed when we get home, for it is not the first time this has happened, and I know what the smell will be like when we are inside the kitchen. But now it is still dark, and I can sit here by Swan Lake thinking about whatever I choose.

15 Now

I WALK BACK UP THE HILL TO MY HOUSE. Daylight breaks in full red and yellow, the temperature rises, I feel it on my face, and no doubt most of the snow will soon melt, maybe already by this evening. No matter what I have said before, that would be a disappointment just now.

There is a car parked in the yard beside mine. I can see it clearly from down the slope, it's a white Mitsubishi Spacewagon, rather like the one I considered buying myself as it looked robust and suited the place I had bought and was going to move to, and that was how I saw my situation then, after I had made my decision; as slightly robust, and I liked that, I felt rather robust myself after three years in a hall of glass where the slightest of movements set everything crackling, and the first shirt I fell for after the move was a red-and-black checked, thick flannel one of a kind I had not worn since the Fifties.

Someone is standing in front of the white Mitsubishi, a lady, by the looks of it, in a dark coat, bare-headed, and her hair is fair and curly for natural or more technical reasons, and she has left the engine running, I can see the exhaust rising noiselessly and white against the darker trees behind the yard. She stands, relaxed, waiting with one hand to her forehead or in her hair, looking down the road to where I am walking up, and there is something about that figure I have seen before, and then Lyra catches sight of her and throws herself forward and runs like the

Daughter
Ellen
Visits

wind towards her. I have not heard any car approaching, and neither did I notice any tyre marks in the snow when I came out on the road from the path, but then I was not expecting any car, not at this time of day. It cannot be more than eight o'clock. I look at my watch and it says half past eight. Ah, well.

It is my daughter standing there. The elder of two. Her name is Ellen. She has lit a cigarette and holds it the way she always has, in stretched fingers away from her body as if she is on the point of giving it to someone else, or pretending it is not hers. That alone would have made me recognise her. I swiftly calculate that she must be thirty-nine now. She is still an attractive lady. I do not think it's me she takes after, but her mother was certainly good looking. I have not seen Ellen for six months at least, and have not spoken to her since I moved, or well before, actually. To be honest, I have not given her much thought, nor her sister, for that matter. There has been so much else. I get to the top of the slope and Lyra is standing in front of Ellen, wagging her tail and having her head patted, and the two of them do not know each other, but she is fond of dogs, and they trust her at once. It has been like that since she was little. I seem to recall she had a dog herself when I went to see her last. A brown dog. That is all I can remember. It's quite a while ago now. I stop and smile my most natural smile and she straightens up and looks at me.

'So it's you,' I say.

'Yes, it is. Did I surprise you?'

'Can't be denied,' I say. 'You're out early.'

She smiles a kind of half smile that soon fades, and

takes a drag on the cigarette, exhales again slowly and holds it away from her body with her arm almost straight out. She is not smiling any more. That rather worries me. She says:

'Early? Maybe it is. Anyway, I slept so badly I thought I might as well get an early start. I left about seven, as soon as the ones supposed to leave the house had actually left. I've given myself a day off, I decided on that long ago. It didn't take me much more than an hour to drive out here. I had expected it to be longer. It felt good, in fact, that it wasn't any further. I just arrived. About fifteen minutes ago.'

'I didn't hear the car,' I said. 'I was in the woods, down there by the lake. There was plenty of snow.' I turn and point, and before I have turned back she has stubbed out her cigarette in my yard and taken the few steps towards me and put her arms round my neck and given me a hug. She smells good and is still the same height. Which is not so strange, you do not grow much between thirty and forty, but there was a time when I was away travelling most of the year, back and forth, back and forth in every possible direction in Norway, and both girls had grown each time I came home, or that is how it seemed to me, and they sat so quietly side by side on the sofa, and I knew they were staring at the door where I would soon come in, and it made me confused, I recall, and uneasy at times, when finally I did come and saw them sitting there, shy and full of expectation. I feel a bit ill at ease now too, for she hugs me hard and says:

'Hi, my old dad. It's good to see you.'

'Hi, my girl, the same to you,' I say, and she does not

let go, but stays in that position and says very softly into my neck:

'I had to call all the town councils for eighty miles around and more to find out where you lived. I've been doing it for weeks. You don't even have a telephone.'

'No, I suppose I haven't.'

'No, you certainly do *not*. Damn you,' she says, and thumps me several times on my back, and not that lightly either. I say:

'Steady on, I'm an old man, remember,' and she may be crying then, but I am not sure. Anyway she is hugging me so hard it's difficult to breathe, and I do not push her away, just go on holding my breath, and I put my arms round her, maybe a bit on the tentative side, and wait like that until she loosens her grip, and then I let my hands sink down and take a step backwards and breathe out.

'You may just as well cut the engine now,' I say, gasping a little and nodding at the Mitsubishi standing there humming faintly. The first rays of sunlight flash on the newly polished white paint and dazzle me. My eyes smart, so I close them for a minute.

'Oh, yes,' she says, 'so I can. You *do* live here. I didn't even recognise your car, I thought maybe I had come to the wrong place.'

I hear her walking round her car in the snow and move a few steps to the side and open my eyes as she opens the car door, leans in and turns the key and switches the lights off. There's full silence. She did weep a little, I can see.

'Come in for a cup of coffee,' I say. 'And I really do need to sit down, my legs are giving out after my walk through the snow. As I said, I'm an old man. Have you had breakfast?'

'No,' she says. 'I didn't take the time.'

'Then we'll have something. Come on.'

Lyra brightens up at the word 'Come' and moves up the two steps to stand in front of the door.

'She's lovely,' my daughter says. 'When did you get her? She's no puppy, is she?'

'Over six months ago. I went to the animal sanctuary outside Oslo where they find new homes for animals. Don't remember the name of the place. I took her at once, there was no doubt, she just came up to me and sat down wagging her tail. She almost offered herself,' I say, trying a small chuckle. 'But they didn't know how old she was, or what breed.'

'It's called the A.R.A., the Association for the Rehoming of Animals. I went there once. It looks as if she's a bit of everything. In England it's called British Standard, which is a nice way of saying they are a mixture of everything you could possibly find in the streets. But she really is lovely. What's her name?'

Ellen went to school in England for a couple of years, and got a lot out of it. But she was grown up then. Before that there were several years when she didn't get much out of anything.

'Her name is Lyra. It wasn't me who thought that up. It said so on the collar she was wearing. Anyway I am glad I chose her,' I say. 'I haven't regretted it for a second. We get on really well, and she makes living alone much easier.'

Those last words sound a bit self-pitying, and disloyal to my life here, I do not need to defend it or explain it to anyone, not even to this daughter of mine, whom I do like a lot, I must say, and she has come out here early in the morning on dark roads through several counties in her Mitsubishi Spacewagon from somewhere right on the outskirts of Oslo, from Maridalen actually, to find out where I live, because I probably have not told her that and have not even given it a thought; that I *should* have done. That may seem strange, I see that now, and her eyes turn moist again, and that irritates me a little.

I open the door and Lyra stays on the doorstep until both Ellen and I are in the hall. Then I let her in with a small well-drilled gesture. I take my daughter's coat and hang it on a free peg and follow her into the kitchen. It is still warm in there. I open the small door to the stove and have a look, and, as I hoped, there are still glowing embers in the firebox.

'This can be saved,' I say, and open the lid of the woodbox and sprinkle some kindling and strips of paper over the embers and then arrange three medium-size logs round them. I open the ash-pan cover to make a draught and straightaway there is a crackle.

'It's nice in here,' she says.

I close up the stove and look around. I don't know if she is right. I had hoped it would be nice in time, when most of my planned improvements have been launched, but it is clean, and tidy. Maybe that was what she meant, that she had expected something else from a single elderly man, and what she saw surprised her in a positive way. If it did, she does not remember much from the time we spent together. Untidiness does not suit me and never has. I am actually a meticulous person; I want everything in its place and ready for use. Dust and mess make me nervous. If I once get slack over cleaning, it is easy to let everything slide, especially in this old house. One of my many horrors is to become the man with the frayed jacket and unfastened flies standing at the Co-op counter with egg on his shirt and more too because the mirror in the hall has given up the ghost. A shipwrecked man without an anchor in the world except in his own liquid thoughts where time has lost its sequence.

I ask her to sit at the table and then I fill the kettle with fresh water for coffee and put it on the cooker, and there is a hissing sound at once. I must have forgotten to switch it off when I used it this morning, and that is really quite serious, but I do not think Ellen took any notice, so I just ignore it and cut some bread, which I put in a basket. I suddenly feel angry and slightly sick, and I see my hand is shaking, so I keep myself at an angle to hide it from her when I pass her to fetch sugar and milk and blue napkins and all that is needed to make this into a meal. I really had my fill a couple of hours ago and am not hungry yet, but even so I set out enough for the both of us, as she might feel embarrassed sitting there eating on her own. After all, it is a long time since we saw each other last. But actually I would rather not, and then there is nothing more to do that I can think of and I have to sit down.

She has been gazing out the window at the view of the lake. I look the same way and say:

'I call it Swan Lake.'

'There are swans on it, then?'

'There certainly are. Two or three families, that I've seen.'

Then she turns to me. 'Tell me. How are you really?' she says, as if there were two versions of my life, and now she is not on the verge of tears at all, but sharp-voiced as an interrogator. She is playing a role, I know, and behind it she is the one she has always been, at least I hope she is; that life has not turned her into an old nag, if I may be forgiven the expression. But I take a deep breath and pull myself together, shove my hands under my thighs on the chair and tell her about my days here, about how well I am doing, with carpentry and chopping wood and my long walks with Lyra, that I have a neighbour I can cooperate with at a pinch, his name is Lars, I say, a clever chap with a chainsaw. We have a lot in common, I say, smiling what is intended to be a secretive smile, but I can see she is not with me there, so I do not take it any further, but tell her I was a bit anxious about all the snow I knew would fall now that winter is really coming, but I have sorted that out, as she can see for herself and must have noticed when she drove up to the house, because I have made an arrangement with a farmer called Åslien. He drives a tractor with a snowplough and can do my clearing when it's needed, at a price of course. So I do get on, I say, and manage a smile, then I listen to the radio, I say, all morning when I'm indoors, and I read in the evening, various things, but mostly Dickens.

She smiles a real smile now, no moist eyes, no sharp edges.

'You were always reading Dickens at home,' she says. 'I remember that well. You in your chair with a book, miles away, and I'd go up to you and pull your sleeve and ask what you were reading, and at first you didn't seem to recognise me, and then you replied "Dickens", with a serious look, and I thought that reading Dickens was not the same as reading other books; that it was something quite unusual, which perhaps not everyone did; that was how it sounded to me. I didn't even know Dickens was the name of the author of the book you were holding. I thought it was a special kind of book that only we possessed. Sometimes you read aloud, I remember.'

'Did I?'

'Yes, you did. From *David Copperfield,* as it turned out, when I was grown up and realised I had to read those books myself. Those days you never seemed to get tired of *David Copperfield.*'

'It's a long time since I last read that one.'

'But you do have it, don't you?'

'Oh, yes, I certainly have.'

'Then I think you should read it again,' she says, and resting her chin in one hand with her elbow on the table she says:

'"Whether I shall turn out to be the hero of my own life, or whether that station will be held by anybody else, these pages must show."'

She smiles again and says: 'I always thought those opening lines were a bit scary because they indicated we would not necessarily be the leading characters of our own lives. I couldn't imagine how that could come about, something so awful; a sort of ghost-life where I could do nothing but watch that person who had taken my place and maybe hate her deeply and envy her everything, but not be able to do anything about it because at some point in time I had fallen out of my life, as if from an aeroplane, I pictured it, and out into empty space, and there I drifted about and could not get back, and someone else was sitting fastened into my seat, although that place was mine, and I had the ticket in my hand.'

It's not easy for me to say anything to that. I didn't know she had been thinking that way. She never told me. For the quite simple reason, of course, that I was not there when she needed to talk, but she can have no idea how often I have had the same thoughts and have read those first lines of *David Copperfield* and then just had to go on, page after page, almost rigid with terror because I had to see if everything fell into its rightful place in the end, and naturally it did, but it always took a long time before I felt safe. In the book. Real life was something different. In real life I have not had the courage to ask Lars the obvious question:

'Did you take the place that was rightfully mine? Did you have years out of my life that I should have lived?'

I never thought my father travelled to countries like South Africa or Brazil or to towns like Vancouver or Montevideo to make a new life for himself. He did not take flight, as so many have done, from actions committed in anger and passion or from a life in ruins after capricious blows of fate, he did not go off head over heels, shielded by the silent summer night with fearful, squinting eyes as Jon did. My father was no sailor. He stayed by the river, of that I am certain. That was what he wished for. And the fact that Lars does not talk about him when he is up at my place, the fact that Lars has not mentioned my father, not one single word in the time we have known each other, must be because he feels he wants to spare me, or because, like myself, he cannot make his thoughts come together around these persons, himself and myself included; come into that one point, because he does not have the words for it. I do understand that. It has been the same for me almost all my life.

But that is not what I want to think about now. I rise quickly from the table, bumping into it on my way up, and making it jolt so the cups jump and coffee spatters over the tablecloth and the yellow cream jug overturns and milk floods out and mixes with the coffee, and a stream runs down, heading for Ellen's lap, and the reason for that is the sloping floor. A difference of five centimetres, in fact, from wall to wall. I measured it long ago. I should have done something about that too, but it is a huge job to lay a new floor. It will have to wait.

Ellen pushes her chair back quickly and gets up before the small stream reaches the edge of the table, and she picks up a corner of the cloth and folds it back and stops the flood with two napkins.

'Sorry. I was in too much of a hurry,' I say and to my surprise I hear the words come out of my mouth in short bursts, as if I had been running and was out of breath.

'Never mind. We just have to get this cloth off promptly so we can rinse it in the sink. No harm's done that a spot of washing powder can't put right.' She takes control of the situation in a way no-one has done in here before, and I make no protest; she has moved everything on the table over to the worktop in no time and puts the cloth under the tap to rinse the stained part and carefully wrings the cloth out and hangs it to dry over a chair in front of the warm wood stove.

'You can put it in the washing machine later on,' she says.

I open the woodbox and put a couple of logs in the stove.

'Actually, I don't have a washing machine,' I say, and it sounds so poverty-stricken when I say it like that, I have to laugh, but that little chuckle does not come out so well, and she takes it in, Ellen, I can see she does. It really is not easy to find the appropriate tone in this situation.

She wipes the table with a cloth she wrings out thoroughly several times under running water as it is full of milk, and you want that well out to prevent the smell, and then she suddenly turns stiff, and with her back to me she says:

'Would you rather I hadn't come?' As if she realised only now that this might be a possibility. But it's a good question. I take a little while to answer. I sit down on the woodbox trying to gather my thoughts, and then she says: 'Perhaps you'd really rather be left in peace? That is why you are out here, isn't it, that's why you have moved to this place, because you want to be in peace, and then here I come bursting into your yard and disturbing you at the crack of dawn, and it wasn't anything you wanted at all, if it was up to you?'

She says all this with her back to me. She has dropped the cloth in the sink and grips the edge of the worktop with both hands, and she does not turn round.

'I have changed my life,' I say. 'That's what's important. I sold what was left of the firm and came out here because I had to, or things would have turned out badly. I couldn't go on the way it was.'

'I understand that,' she says. 'I really do. But why didn't you tell us?'

'I don't know. It's the truth.'

'Would you rather I hadn't come?' she says again, insistently.

'I don't know,' I say, and that is also true; I don't know what to think of her coming out here, it was not part of my plan, and then it strikes me: now she will go away and never come back. That thought fills me with such sudden terror that I quickly say:

'No, that's not true. Don't go.'

'I had no intention of going,' she says then, and only now turns from the sink. 'Not yet anyway, but I would like to make a suggestion.'

'What's that, then?'

'Get yourself a telephone.'

'I'll think about it,' I say. 'Honestly, I will.'

She stays for several hours, and when she gets into her car it has already started to get dark again. By then she has been for a walk with Lyra, at her own choice, while I had half an hour's rest in bed. My house is different now, and the yard is different. She starts up with the door open. She says:

'So now I know where you live.'

'That's good,' I say. 'I'm glad you do,' and she waves briefly and slams the car door and it starts to roll down the slope. I go up the steps and turn off the yard light and walk through the hall to the kitchen. Lyra is at my heels, but even when she is behind me the room feels a bit empty. I look out at the yard, but there is nothing but my own reflection in the dark glass.

AFTER THE TIMBER HAD BEEN SENT OFF, Franz often came down the road to our place. He had granted himself a holiday, he said with a laugh. Wearing shorts he sat on the flagstone outside the door with a cigarette and a cup of coffee, looking odd with his white legs. The sky was just blue and blue; you could say it had gone from light blue to unrelenting blue in record time, and for my part a little rain would have been welcome now.

It probably would have been to my father as well. He was still acting restless. He might go down to the river with a book and lie there to read, in the moored rowing boat with a cushion under his neck against the rear thwart, or on the sloping rocks beneath the cross pine, and it seemed as if he did not give a thought to what had happened in that very place on a winter's day in 1944, or in fact perhaps he did, and then forced himself to look unmoved in order to demonstrate how a man could appear who had a calm and balanced mind and just enjoyed his day. But he did not fool anyone. He was really thinking about the timber, I could see it by the way he raised his head and the look he sent downriver, and it provoked me, that to him it was so important. We had a pact, didn't we? I was there, and we ought to get on with what was left of the summer before it was over and gone forever.

———

The day after we arrived here on the bus he had proposed a three-day outing on horseback, did I not think that a good idea? And when I asked which horses he had in mind he replied: Barkald's horses, and I was enthusiastic and thought it an *extremely* good idea. Now I had stolen a march on him with those horses, but we did not have much of a ride, Jon and I, up there in the forest, and it really did not end up too well, not for me anyway, and not for Jon either if you think about what had happened just before and how everything turned out afterwards, and anyway I had not heard anything about the proposition since that day. So I was quite surprised when I opened my eyes one morning to hear snorting, stamping noises through the open window from the meadow behind the house, where I had done such a miserable job and had not dared cut down the nettles with the short scythe because I was afraid that it would hurt. And then my father had just pulled them up with his bare hands, saying: 'You decide yourself when it will hurt.'

Now I leaned out of the bunk until I hung over the window, supporting my hands on the sill, and with my face close to the glass I could see there were two horses grazing in the meadow. One was a bay and the other black, and I saw at once they were the same two that Jon and I had ridden, and whether that was a good sign or rather a bad one I could not have said that morning if anyone had thought to ask me.

I jumped down from the bunk as usual and landed on the floor perfectly without any damage to my leg or anything else. My knee was better now, it only took a couple of days, and I leaned out the window as far as I could without toppling over. There I saw my father com-

ing from the shed with a saddle in his arms and hanging
it over the saw-horse so the stirrups dangled on each side,
and I called:

'Have you been out *stealing* those horses?' He stopped
and went stiff for a moment before he turned round and
saw me hanging out the window, and when he realised I
was only fooling he smiled and said loudly:

'Get yourself out here on the dot.'

'Aye, aye, chief,' I shouted.

I picked up my clothes from the chair and ran into the
living room and got dressed as quickly as I could without stopping, and I hopped first on one leg and then on
the other as I pulled my trousers on and barely stopped to
step into my gym shoes before coming half blind out onto
the steps with my shirtsleeves flapping above my head.
When my face finally surfaced I could see him standing
by the door of the shed staring at me and laughing heart-
ily at what he saw, and in his arms he had another saddle.

'This one's for you,' he said. 'If you're still interested,
that is. You were before, I remember.'

'Of course I'm interested,' I said. 'Are we going now?
Where to?'

'Never mind where to, breakfast comes first,' said my
father. 'And then we have to make the horses ready. That
takes some time, it has to be done properly, it's not just
a matter of going. We have them on loan for three days
to the minute. You know Barkald, he doesn't mess around
with his possessions. I don't even understand why he said
yes.'

But that was no mystery to me. Barkald liked my father
and always had done, and according to what Franz had
told me, the state of confidence between them was stron-

ger than I had first imagined. Maybe my father had not
even paid for our place, maybe Barkald had just let him
have it because they were such great friends when the war
was over on account of the things they had gone through
together. Then everything was altogether different, wasn't
it, from when we came here for the first time, and the forest and the river were strange to me, and the yard by the
shop was new, and the bridge was new, and I had never
seen logs moving yellow and glittering on the current of
a river, and Barkald was a man I looked on with suspicion
because he had property and money, and we did not, and
I thought my father felt the same way. But obviously he
did not, and when he said what he said now, it must have
been to make light of the situation or to throw a veil over
the real state of things.

In that case, it all seemed a bit dubious, but I could not
dwell on it now, because summer would soon be over, at
least for us. And the heaviness I felt inside on the timber-
launching day that weighed me down and almost ruined
my knee was mysteriously lifted from my body and had
vanished. Now I felt as restless as my father and was in-
tent on squeezing everything possible out of the days we
had left and out of the river and the landscape around it
before we went back to Oslo.

And that was what we set out to do: wring the last warmth
from the paths through the forest and the high ridges in
the sunshine on the Furufjellet and see the reflection of
dazzling birch boles swirling through the trees like arrows shot from the bows of the Kiowas diving into deep
green ferns swaying at the sides of the narrow gravel path
like palm leaves on Palm Sunday in the Sunday School

Bible. We walked the horses down the path from our cabin, past the old wooden barn I had spent a night in not long ago and suddenly felt the heat in my body, now being the heat from the horse's flanks against my thighs, and against my face the warmth of the wind from the south. We rode to meet it on our own east side of the river, and we had had breakfast and packed the saddle-bags and rolled up rugs to keep us warm sleeping outdoors, and the anoraks were tied up with the rugs, and the horses were groomed and their manes shining. Above the ridge to the west, banks of cloud were sailing along the top, but there would be no rain, my father had said, shaking his head and just swinging into the saddle.

Down there outside the barn the dairymaid was washing her buckets and tubs in the stream with water and soda, and the sun flashed in the metal and in the icily clear water pouring into the buckets and splashing out again, and we waved to her, and she raised her hand and waved back, and a shining streak of water flew up in an arc through the air before it fell to the ground. The horses snorted and tossed their heads, and she laughed aloud when she saw who it was passing by, but there was no malice there, and I did not blush.

She had a nice voice, and it might well have sounded like a silver flute for all I knew, and my father turned in his saddle and looked at me riding close behind him. I was still busy finding a way of sitting in the saddle that felt right. 'Let your hips go loose,' my father had said. 'Let your hips be a part of the horse. You have a ball-bearing there,' he said. 'Use that,' and I knew he was right, that my body was put together in such a way that it was good for riding, if I wanted it to be.

'Do you know *her* as well?' my father said now.

'Sure I do, we know each other well,' I said. 'I've been to see her several times,' which was not strictly true, but I didn't know who else he was referring to when he said 'her as well', whether it was Jon's mother he meant, and the way he said it made me wonder if he was still angry with me after the day we sent the timber off, and then he said:

'What about someone your own age?'

'There isn't anyone here,' I said, and that at least was true. In two summers I had not seen a girl of my age for several kilometres around, and that was fine by me. I had no time for someone my own age, what did I want with her? It was fine as it was, and I heard my voice getting stiff and hostile, and he looked me straight in the eye and then he smiled.

'You're damn well right there,' he said and turned back, and I heard him laugh.

'What are you laughing at?' I shouted and felt myself getting mad, but he did not turn round, just said into the air:

'I'm laughing at myself.' At least I think that's what he said, and it may well have been true. He could certainly do that, laugh at himself. Something I was no good at, while he often did. But why he should do so just now, I did not understand. Then he gently touched his horse's sides with his heels and it picked up speed to an easy trot.

'Let's go,' he called, and riding behind him I had plenty to take care of, making the ball-bearings in my hips roll correctly in the saddle when my horse too broke into a trot and followed, and the barn disappeared among the trees behind us, and the dairymaid stayed there in the yard with her shining brown knees under her skirt and her strong brown arms in the air.

We went on down the road until it narrowed into a path, but we did not follow the bend across the straight near the river and the jetty in the rushes where I had walked one night in a strange light and seen my father kissing Jon's mother as if it was the last thing he would ever do. Instead we went on along another path that soon turned eastwards and gradually shrank into no more than a zigzagging moose track through tall old birches with great swishing crowns when you put your head back and gazed up through the foliage, and I did that until I had a crick in my neck and tears in my eyes, and we crossed a deep stream whose water looked icy cold. And it *was* cold when it splashed up between the horses' legs and over my thighs immediately soaking my trousers, and a few drops even hit my face when we splashed over at a trot, and the horses liked that; the terrain changing as we came closer to the Furufjellet. The spruce forest was dense and untouched by loggers on the steep mountain-sides, and we followed the track to the top of the ridge and stopped for a moment at the highest point and turned the horses to look back, and the river wound a dull silver through the treetops between newly mown meadows, and the cloud banks lay above the ridge on the other side of the valley. It was grand to look at, better than the fjord at home. I did not really give a damn about the fjord, to tell the truth, and now was the last time for ages I would be able to look out over the valley here like this, that I knew, and it did not make me melancholy as you might think, but irritated almost, and a little angry. I wanted to go on. I felt my father was sitting there longer than necessary, facing west, and then I turned my horse with its back to the valley and said:

'We can't stay hanging about here.'

He looked at me and smiled faintly, and then he too turned his horse and started to move straight for the east where I knew Sweden was. When we got there it would all look exactly as it did on this side of the border, but it would feel different, I was sure of that, because I had never been in Sweden. If that was where we were going. My father had not said anything about it. I just assumed we were.

And I was not mistaken. We came down from the ridge on the other side through a narrow pass with our view blocked to all sides, and the horses stepped cautiously down the path, picking their way through the pebbles and loose stones that covered the slope, and it was steep too. So I leaned back in the saddle keeping my legs straight and my feet pressed hard down in the stirrups so as not to tumble over the horse's neck and down the slope, and the noise of the iron-clad hooves rang between the rocks on both sides of the pass and there were echoes too, so you would not say we moved quietly along. But it did not matter, I thought, for there was no-one chasing us now, no German patrol with machine gun and binoculars, no border police with tracker dogs, no lean and thin-lipped U.S. Marshall on an equally lean horse did follow us, day in and day out, keeping his distance, no closer, no further away, patiently waiting for the moment when our nerves were worn to shreds and we for a moment forgot to be on our guard. Then he would strike. Without hesitation. Without mercy.

I turned round cautiously in the saddle and glanced

back to make sure he really was not there on that skinny grey horse of his, and I listened as hard as I could, but the sound of our own horses was far too loud in that narrow cleft to allow us to hear anything else.

At the end of the slope we came out on a plain, and with the shadow of the ridge behind us and the sun on our backs the horses began to trot with sheer relief, and my father pointed at a hillock with a solitary and crooked pine on its top, and he shouted:

'Can you see the pine up there?'

There was not much else to see just here, so I shouted back:

'Of course I can see it.'

'That's where Sweden begins!' and he still pointed at the pine as if it was hard to make out.

'Alright,' I yelled. 'Then it's first man to the pine tree!' and dug my heels into the horse's side; it immediately changed pace and threw itself forward, and I lost hold of the reins and fell almost straight backwards out of the saddle from the sudden jerk, rolled over the horse's rump and crashed onto the ground. Behind me my father shouted:

'Fantastic! One more time! Da Capo!' then he set off at a gallop and passed me by with a loud laugh, chasing the runaway horse. After only a hundred metres he caught up with it, and he bent forward and seized the reins at full speed and made a big semicircle on the flat ground and came pacing back in a way that told the whole world this too was something he could do. But the whole world was not there, it was only me lying flat like an empty sack in the tall grass seeing him come towards me with the two horses, and it did not hurt much anywhere just then, but

I stayed down on my back all the same. He dismounted, came right up and squatted in front of me and said:

'I'm sorry I laughed, it just looked so damn comical, like something in a circus. I know it wasn't funny for you. It was incredibly stupid of me to laugh. Does it hurt a lot anywhere?'

'Not really,' I said.

'Only a little bit in your soul?'

'Maybe a bit.'

'Let it sink, Trond,' he said. 'Just leave it. You can't use it for anything.'

He stretched out a hand to pull me up, and I took it, and he squeezed it so hard it almost hurt, but he did not pull me up. Instead he suddenly sank to his knees, threw his arms round me and pulled me close to his chest. I didn't know what the hell to say, I was really surprised. Of course we were good friends, had been anyway, and no doubt would be again. He was the grown man I looked up to most of all, and we did still have a pact, I was convinced we did, but we were not in the habit of hugging. We could have mock fights and hold round each other doing that and roll back and forth like two idiots over the hillock on the farm where there was room enough for such childish play, but this was not fighting. On the contrary. He had never done such a thing before that I could remember, and it did not feel right. But I let him hold me while I wondered where I should put my hands, for I did not want to push him away, but neither could I hold my arms around him like he did around me, and so I just left them hanging in the air. But I didn't have to think about it for long, because then he let me go and stood up and took my hand again and pulled me onto my feet.

He was smiling now, but I didn't know if it was for me, and I had no idea what to say. He just gave me the reins of my horse, tidily brushed some dirt off my shirt, and was quite his usual self again.

'We'd better get ourselves into Sweden,' he said, 'before the whole country sinks and is lost to us, and then there will just be the Gulf of Bothnia left and Finland on the other side, and we haven't much use for Finland just now.' I did not understand a word that he said, but then he put his foot in the stirrup and swung himself up, and so did I. I did not even try to look elegant, feeling stiff and sore all over, and we climbed at a walk up to the crooked pine that looked like a sculpture and across the border and into Sweden, and it was right what I had expected, that it *felt* different although everything looked the same after we had crossed.

That night we slept under an overhanging cliff, where fires had been made before. We found the remains of two heaps of spruce twigs made into beds to lie on, but all the needles had turned brown and dropped off a long time ago, so we cleared the old ones away and cut new branches from nearby trees with the little axe I had used earlier with such eagerness, and we made up the branches and twigs into two soft beds under the cliff, and it smelled good and strong when you lay down with your face almost buried in it. We fetched our blankets and lit a bonfire in the stone circle and sat on each side of the flames to eat. We had tied our ropes together into a single long one and tied it round four spruce trees with enough distance between them to make a corral, and there we turned the horses loose. From where we sat by the fire we could only just hear them moving around on the soft forest floor and then quite clearly when their hooves struck a stone, and in their throats they made soft sounds to each other, but we could not see them clearly, for it was August now and the evenings were darker. The flames made reflections in the rocky ceiling above me that coloured my thoughts far into sleep and made my dreams more intense, and when I woke in the night I did not remember anything at first about where I was or why. But the fire was still burning and there was glow enough and light from the flames and the coming day to get up and carefully walk down to the horses and then recover my memory, all in one slow stream while roots and pebbles scraped the soles of my feet, and I talked to the horses over the rope very quietly about quiet things I forgot the moment I had spoken them, and I stroked up and down their powerful necks. Afterwards I could smell their scent on my fingers and feel in my chest how calm I was before going off to do behind a boulder what I had woken up to do. On my way back I was so sleepy I stumbled several times, and under the overhang I quickly pulled the blanket over me and was gone at once.

Those days were the last days. When I sit here now, in the kitchen of the old house I have planned to make into a liveable place in the years left to me, and my daughter has gone after a surprising visit and taken with her her voice and her cigarettes and the orange lights from her car down the road, and I look back to that time, I see how each movement through the landscape took colour from what came afterwards and cannot be separated from it. And when someone says the past is a foreign country, that they do things differently there, then I have probably felt that way for most of my life because I have been obliged to, but I am not any more. If I just concentrate I can walk into memory's store and find the right shelf with the right film and disappear into it and still feel in my body that ride through the forest with my father; high above the river along the ridge and then down on the other side, across the border into Sweden and far into what *was* a foreign country, at least for me. I can lean back and sit by the bonfire under the overhanging cliff as I was that night when I woke up a second time and saw my father lying with his eyes open, staring up into the rock above him; quite still with his hands under his head and a red light from the embers on his forehead and stubbly cheek, and although I should have liked to I was not awake long enough to see if he actually did close his eyes before the morning came. Nevertheless he was up long before me and had watered the horses and groomed them both, and was keen to get going; he moved around tensely, but there was no sharpness in his voice that I could hear. Then we packed up and saddled the horses before the dreams had left my mind and were on our way before I could think anything apart from very simple thoughts.

I heard the river before I could see it, and we rounded a small hill and there it was, almost white through the trees, and something in the air changed which made it easier to breathe. I could see straightaway that it was our own river, just further south and well inside Sweden, and even if it's not possible to recognise water from the way it flows, that was precisely what I did.

Soon we were down at the bank and moving the horses southwards as well as we could, and my father scanned up and downriver and across to the other side, and at first we saw only one single log rammed against a bed of rushes, and then several that were stuck on a shoal further down. My father fetched his axe then and cut some strong poles from two small pine trees, and we waded out in our shoes; I in my gym shoes and my father in his heavy lace-up boots, and we used the poles for timber stakes and sent the logs back into the current. But I could see he was worried now, for the water level was not much to boast about, and certainly not for rafting timber, and he wanted to get further down the river at once. So we mounted the horses and rode off with the long poles like lances pointing to the sky at the horses' sides like Ivanhoe and his knights must have held their lances going to a tournament or a decisive battle against the treacherous Normans in the England of old. I tried to keep my imagination in check, but it was not easy on horseback, riding through the thickets alongside the bank, because the enemy could appear at any moment. We came to a bend in the river, and once round it there was a stretch of rapids where a log had wedged itself right in midstream between two large rocks that were bare and dry in the sinking water, and more and more logs had come drifting and piled up against the first one. Now there was a large stack out there, firmly wedged. That was not what my father wanted to see. He seemed to collapse in his saddle, and it pained me to see him like that, and it made me uneasy, so I jumped off my horse and ran down to the water and gazed out at the tangle of timber, and I ran some way along the bank still staring out into the river and ran back again, and then even further, and I hopped about unable to stand still and studied the jumble from every possible angle. Finally I called to my father:

'If we get a rope round that log there'—I pointed to the one that held the key to the problem—'and haul it just a *little* way from the rock, it will break loose from the jam, and then the rest is sure to follow.'

'It won't be easy to get out there,' he said, and his voice now was flat and unenthusiastic. 'And we won't be able to haul that log one millimetre,' he said.

'That's right, we won't,' I shouted. 'But the horses will.'

'OK,' he said, and I felt a surge of relief. I ran over to my horse and untied the rope from the saddle, and then my father's rope, and tied the two together and put a slip-knot at one end and pulled it tight and eased it over my head and under my armpits across my chest, and tightened it a little behind my back.

'You have to look after the other end,' I shouted without turning round to see whether he would accept a direct order, and then I ran up the bank as far as I thought was enough, and there threw myself straight in to get the shock over with. At first I almost crawled along the bed, and then it suddenly grew deep and I began to swim out to the middle of the river. The current was not strong here, but it pulled me with it all the same, and then I was all the way out and at once moving faster. I let myself drift until my hands met the first log, and I felt it to see if it held and hoisted myself up, and the soles of my gym shoes found a foothold on the trunk. I stood there swaying until everything felt right, and then I began to jump from log to log, holding the rope high in one hand, jumping up and down the tangled timber and across to the other side and back again, and I took a few quite un-

necessary leaps to get the rhythm in my legs, and to feel
if it was still inside me, and some logs spun round when
I landed on them and shifted their position, but I had already moved on and did not lose my balance, and my father called from the bank:

'What are you doing out there?'

'I'm flying!' I shouted back.

'When did you learn to do that?' he shouted.

'When you weren't looking,' I called, and laughed and
leaped right forward to the log that was causing the trouble
and there I saw that the end that I wanted the rope round
was well under water.

'I'll have to go down there,' I shouted. And before my
father could say anything, I had jumped in and let myself
sink until I stood on the riverbed. There I felt the current
punch me in the back and pull at my arms, and I opened
my eyes and saw the end of the trunk straight in front
of me, got the loop over my head and fastened it where
I wanted it to be. It all went so well I felt I could stand
there a long time almost weightless and just hold my
breath and keep my hands around that log. But then I let
go and rose to the surface. My father tightened the rope,
and all I needed to do was haul myself in to the bank. I
stood up dripping on dry land, and my father said:

'Goddamn it, that was not bad,' and then he
smiled and tied the rope to the harness with a make-
shift measure he had constructed while I was out in
the river, and picked up the reins and stepped in front
of the horse and shouted Pull! And the horse pulled
as hard as it could, and nothing happened. Again he
shouted Pull! And the horse pulled, and then we heard

a scraping sound out from the rapids, and it was as if something broke, and the whole pile of timber tipped forwards. Log after log slid off and was seized by the current on the lower side of the rapids. My father looked almost happy then, and I could see by the way he looked at me that I did too.

III

17

IT WAS AS IF A CURTAIN HAD FALLEN, hiding everything I had ever known. It was almost like being born again. The colours were different, the smells different, the feeling things gave you right down inside yourself was different. Not just the difference between heat, cold; light, darkness; purple, grey. But the difference in the way I was frightened and the way I was happy.

And I was happy from time to time, even in those first weeks after I left the cabin by the river. I was happy and full of expectation when I got on my bike and coasted down the steep Nielsenbakken, past Ljan Station and on to Mosseveien to ride the seven kilometres into central Oslo, but at the same time I was restless and might laugh out loud for no reason, and found it hard to concentrate. Everything I saw along the road and the fjord were things I had always known, yet nothing was the same. Not Nesodden or the Bunnefjord in towards the beach at Ingierstrand and the Roald Amundsen house, not Ulv Island with the nice bridge from the road across the narrow sound, or Malm Island immediately behind it, not the grain silo on Vippetangen Pier or the grey walls of the fortress on the other side of the harbour basin where the liner for America tied up. Nor the late August sky over the city.

I can see myself cycling all the way to the Østbane Station in the almost white sunlight; grey shorts and open shirt, fluttering past Bekkelaget; the railway line to the

left here and the fjord to the left and the steep rocky hillside of the Ekeberg ridge on the right; the scream of gulls,
the creosote scent of the railway sleepers and the raw scent
of salt water in the quivering air. It was still hot at the end
of August although the summer was really over, a heat-
wave almost, and I could pedal at my top speed with the
burning air pouring against my bare chest where sweat
was running or just sail dry-skinned along under the
sun and sometimes hear myself sing.

My father had given me that bicycle the year before
when you could not find a single new one anywhere in
the country. He had had it for years, but had left it in the
basement for long periods of time because he was hardly
ever at home, and he had no use for it any more; the times
were new, he said, with new plans, and the bicycle was
not part of those plans. It was probably just something
he said, but I was glad to have it and looked after it well.
It gave me a freedom and a range I would not have done
without. I had several times taken it to pieces and reassem-
bled it the way my father had shown me. It was washed
and polished and oiled in all its joints and cogwheels,
and the chain ran smoothly round and round without a
sound from the crank with the pedals to the hub in the
back wheel and back again in the brightly polished chain
guard, from the moment I got on and free wheeled down
the hill from home until just as soundlessly I turned in
on the sea side of Østbane Station and parked it there in a
cycle rack and once again walked through the tall doors
out of the sharp sunlight and into the dim, dust-filled
air of the concourse to study the arrivals board. I walked
along the barriers among a crowd of other people looking at the signs in front of the various platforms where the

soot-laden glass roof arched high above the people and the trains, but probably I was the only one who pulled at the sleeve of a uniformed conductor and asked in detail about every single train arriving in Oslo by way of Elverum. He gave me a long look, he knew me, I had asked him before, many times, and he only pointed up to the signs I had already seen. No secret information was available, no sign mislaid anywhere.

As usual I was too early. I took up my position beside a pillar to wait in the strange half-light that was the same at all times of the day in the huge station concourse and yet never quite right for any of them; not for day or evening, not for morning, and not for night either; and there were echoes from people's shoes and people's voices, and most of all there was a great silence high up under the roof where the pigeons sat in long rows, grey and white and pied brown, looking down at me. They had nests everywhere between the iron girders and made their homes there all their lives.

But of course he did not come.

I do not know how many times I made that journey during the late summer of 1948 to wait for the train from Elverum. And each time I felt as tense and expectant, indeed almost happy when I got on my bike and set off down the Nielsenbakken and all the way in, to stand there waiting.

But of course he did not come.

And then came the long-awaited rain, and I went on cycling into Oslo almost every other day to see if he was on the train from Elverum *that* particular day. I wore my sou'wester and my oilskins, I looked like a fisherman from Lofoten in my yellow outfit, and I had Wellingtons, and the water splashed out on either side of the wheels. It came gushing down the hillside under the Ekeberg ridge and onto the railway line on the right side of the road before the rails vanished into a tunnel and popped out again on the left side a little further on, and all the houses and buildings were greyer than they had ever been and vanished in the rain, with no eyes, no ears, no voices, they told me nothing any more. And then I stopped. One day I did not go in, nor the next day, or the day after that. It was as if a curtain had fallen. It was like being born again. The colours were different, the smells different, the feeling things gave you right down inside yourself was different. Not just the difference between heat, cold; light, darkness; purple, grey, but the difference in the way I was frightened and the way I was happy.

Late that autumn a letter arrived. It was postmarked Elverum, and my mother's name was on the envelope, and the address on the Nielsenbakken was there, but on the sheet of notepaper inside all our three names were written, our surname too, although we had the same one. It looked odd. It was a short letter. He thanked us for the time we had spent together, he looked back on it with happiness, but times were different now, and it could not be helped: he was not coming home any more. In a bank in Karlstad, Sweden, there was money due for the timber we had felled that summer and sent downriver. He had already written to the bank, and he now enclosed an authorisation for my mother to draw that money by going to Karlstad with proof of her identity. Best wishes. End. No special greeting to me. I don't know. I really thought I had earned one.

'Timber?' was the only thing my mother said. She was already showing that heaviness in her body she would keep for the rest of her life, not merely a heaviness in arms and hips and the way she walked, but a heaviness in her voice and her whole bearing, even her eyelids had grown heavy, as if she were falling asleep and not fully conscious, and the thing was that I had never said a word to her about what we had been up to, my father and I, that summer. Not a word. Only that he would come home as soon as he could, when what he had to sort out was finished.

My mother borrowed money from the brother who had not been shot by the Gestapo while trying to escape from a police station on the south coast in 1943. We called him Uncle Amund. The one who was shot was Uncle Arne. They had been twins. They had stayed together through everything, gone to school together, gone cross-country skiing together, gone hunting together, but now Uncle Amund was a lonely hunter. He lived in the flat he and Arne had shared in the city, in Vålerenga. He had not married. He could not have been more than thirty-one or two then, but there was a smell of old man in his flat in Smålensgata, at least I thought so when I went to visit him there.

With the money she borrowed she bought tickets to Karlstad on the Stockholm train. I had studied the route: departure early in the morning from Oslo Øst, up along the Glomma river to Kongsvinger, then sharply to the south across the border to Sweden and Charlottenberg and down to Arvika by the Glafsfjord and on in the same direction towards Karlstad, the capital of Wärmland district, beside the great lake Vänern, so big in fact that

Karlstad was a port. Return the same afternoon. My mother wanted me to go with her, while my sister stayed at home. Typical, my sister said, and she was right enough, but that was bloody well not my doing.

This time it was not a bicycle ride along Mosseveien to the Østbane Station, but the local train from Ljan beside the fjord, and on the fjord it was no longer summer but a low grey sky almost touching the tops of the waves and a violent wind that whipped the water into white lace between the islands. I stood on the platform and watched a lady's hat come flying high above the railway line, and the tall pine trees which were so plentiful out where we lived swayed in the wind and bent eerily down in the worst gusts. But they did not fall. Many times when I was small I thought they would, that they would tumble right over with their roots in the air, as I sat by the window on the first floor gazing nervously at the slim reddish-yellow trunks being harried everywhere by the wind among the houses in the hills above the fjord, and they leaned perilously, but they never fell.

At the Østbane Station I knew at once which platform every train arrived at, I knew when every train was leaving, and I walked my mother to the correct platform and found the correct coach and to my right and my left I greeted people I had talked to before; porters and conductors and the lady in the kiosk and two men who hung about in there only to drink something revolting, unrecognisable, from a bottle they shared, and every day they were chased out, and every day just as regularly they came back.

I sat in the compartment by the window facing backwards, because my mother could not sit that way without feeling sick, she said, and lots of people have the same problem but it did not worry me in the least. The train sped along the Glomma, and the poles ticked past outside by Blaker Station and by Årnes; ping and ping and ping, and the wheels beat against the rail joints; dungadung, dungadung, dungadung, and I slept where I sat with a flickering light on my eyelids; not sunlight, but a greyish-white light from the sky above the water, and I dreamed I was going to the cabin by the river, that it was actually the bus I was sitting in.

I woke up and looked blearily out at the Glomma and knew it was still within me; I was friends with water, with running water, it was a call from the big river that was swelling away in the opposite direction from the one that we were travelling in, for we were going north, and the river ran south towards the towns of the coast, flowing heavily and wide as great rivers always do.

I turned my gaze from the Glomma to my mother sitting opposite me, and to her face where the light flickered on and off with the masts and poles beside the rails and with small bridges and with trees. Her eyes were closed, and the heavy eyelids rested on the round cheeks as if everything save sleeping was unnatural to this face, and I thought; for Christ's sake, he just disappeared and left me with her.

Oh, I did love my mother, I am not saying I didn't, but what future I could read in the face before me was not what I had imagined. Merely to look at that face for longer than three minutes made the world push at my shoulders from both sides. It made me short of breath. I could not sit still. I got up from my seat, pulled the door open and went out into the corridor to the windows on the other side of the train where the fields rushed past and had been harvested already and stood bare and brownish-yellow in the dull autumn light. A man was there looking at the landscape. There was something about his back. He smoked a cigarette and was far gone. When I came to the window he turned as if in a dream and nodded in a friendly way and smiled. He did not look like my father at all. I walked up the corridor alongside the compartment doors to the end of the carriage and turned round at the big water container on the wall and went back again, past the man with the cigarette, and I stared at the floor and went right on to the other end, and there I found an empty compartment. I went in and closed the door and sat down by the window facing the way we were travelling and looked out at the river that came flowing towards me now and disappeared behind my back, and maybe I did cry a little with my face against the pane. Then I closed my eyes and slept like a stone until the conductor wrenched the door open with a crash and said we had arrived at Karlstad. We stood shoulder to shoulder on the platform. The train on the rails behind us was not moving now, but soon it would start up again and hammer away on its journey to Stockholm. We heard snarling from a ventilator, we heard the wind singing in the cables running between telegraph poles alongside the station, and a man on the platform yelled at his wife: 'Come on, goddamn it!' in Swedish, but she stood where she was, surrounded by their luggage. My mother looked lost, her face swollen with sleep. She had never been to another country before. Only I had, but that was in the forest. Karlstad was different from Oslo. They talked differently here, we heard that at once, and not only the words but the intonation sounded foreign. The town seemed better arranged than Oslo, viewed from the station, and it looked much less shabby. But we did not know where to go. We had only one bag with us, as we had no intention of spending the night there or of making any long excursions. We really only wanted to get to the bank, the Wärmlandsbank, as it was called, which was somewhere in the centre of this town, and then we would want something to eat. We thought we could just about afford that; to eat in a café just for once after we had been to the bank to collect the money my father left us, but I knew my mother had made a packed lunch and put it in the bag for safety.

We went over to the station building and through it across the tiled floor and then over the road outside that ran alongside the railway. We walked up Järnvägsgatan and to the town centre. We looked at the houses on either side for the nameplate of the bank, whose address was on a letter in the bag, but we could not find it, and we kept asking each other at intervals: 'Can *you* see it?' And then we said 'No' the one to the other.

I was the one carrying the bag under my arm as we walked the whole length of the street until it came to a halt at the Klara river, which came flowing from the north and from the great forests there and here was divided by a spit of land. We were standing on that spit now, and the river swept down through Karlstad splitting the town into three before finally flowing delta-like out into the great Vänern lake.

'Isn't it lovely?' my mother said, and I guess it was, but it was cold too, with a current of icy air from the river. I was frozen through, having slept on the train and then gone straight into the autumn chill and the wind, and I felt like getting it over with, what we had come for:

the settling of the account once and for all, and someone to draw two lines under the columns: this much you
had. This much you gave away. This much you have left.

We turned from the river and went down another street
parallel to the one we had walked up.

'Are you cold?' my mother said. 'There's a scarf in the
bag you can have. It's not a lady's scarf or anything, so you
needn't be ashamed.'

'No, I'm not cold,' I said, and heard an impatient
and irritated edge in my voice. I have been criticised
for that later in life, by women especially, and that is
because it is women I have used it against. I admit it.

A moment later I pulled it out of the bag. It had belonged to my father, but I just put it round my neck and
tied it under my chin and pushed the long ends flat down
inside my jacket so they covered most of my chest. I felt
immediately better and said firmly:

'We have to ask someone. We can't just wander round
the streets like this.'

'Oh, we're sure to find it,' my mother said.

'Sure we will, in the end, but it's stupid to take so
much time over it.'

I knew she was afraid people would not understand
her if she asked them, that it would confuse her and make
her look helpless, like a peasant woman in the city, she
had once said, and she wanted to avoid that at all costs. To
my mother, country folk were a backward segment of the
population.

'Then I will ask someone,' I said.

'You go ahead if you want to. But we'll soon find it in
any case,' she said. 'It must be somewhere hereabouts.'

Blah, blah, blah, I thought, and went over to the first

man coming along the pavement and asked if he could help us find the Wärmlandsbank. He looked perfectly normal and certainly was no drunk; he was well dressed and his coat fairly new. I am sure my choice of words was plain and clear and properly pronounced, but he only looked at me with his mouth open, as if I had come from China and had a pointy hat and slanting eyes, or maybe just one eye in the middle, right above my nose, like the Cyclops I had read about. Suddenly I felt anger shooting up like a blazing column in my chest, my face turned hot, and my throat hurt. I said:

'Are you deaf, or what?'

'What?' It sounded like a dog barking.

'Are you deaf?' I said. 'Don't you listen when people talk to you? Is there something wrong with your ears? Can you tell us where to find the Wärmlandsbank? We have to find that bank. Don't you see?'

He did not understand. He did not understand what I said at all. It was ridiculous. He simply glared at me as he slowly turned his face from side to side with a nervous look in his eyes as if the person in front of him was an idiot escaped from the asylum, and the only thing now was to get through the time it took for the warders to come and drag him back before anyone got hurt.

'Do you want a punch on your mouth?' I said. If he wasn't going to understand what I said I might as well say whatever crossed my mind. Besides, I was as tall as he was and in good shape after that summer, for I had used my body for all kinds of things. I had stretched it and bent it in all directions and lifted and pushed just about everything and hauled and tugged at stone and wood and rowed the boat both up and down the river, I had pedalled the distance between the Nielsenbakken and the Østbane Station countless times through the late summer. Now I felt strong and in a way invincible, and this man did not exactly look an athlete, but he may have understood the last sentence better than the first ones, because his eyes grew round as saucers and were suddenly on their guard. I repeated the offer:

'If you want a punch on your mouth you can have it now, because I certainly feel like giving you one,' I said. 'You've only got to say.'

'No,' he said.

'No what?' I said.

'No,' he said, 'I *don't* want a punch on my mouth. If you hit me, I'll call the police.' He spoke very clearly, like an actor. It made me wildly irritated.

'We'll soon find out,' I said and felt one hand clenching automatically. It felt warm and good and tight in all its joints, and I did not know where they came from, the words I heard myself say. I had never said anything like them to anyone, not to people I knew and certainly not to people I did not know. And it dawned on me that from that small patch of cobble stones I stood on there were lines going out in several directions, as in a precisely drawn diagram, with me standing in a circle in the middle, and today, more than fifty years later, I can close my eyes and clearly see those lines, like shining arrows, and if I did not see them quite as clearly that autumn day in Karlstad, I did know they were there, of that I am certain. And those lines were the different roads I could take, and having chosen one of them, the portcullis would come crashing down, and someone hoist the drawbridge up, and a chain reaction would be set in motion which no-one could stop, and there would be no running back, no retracing my steps. And if I hit the man standing in front of me I would have made that choice.

'Bloody idiot,' I said, and immediately knew I had decided to leave him be. My right fist relaxed itself painfully, and a distinct wave of disappointment crossed the face in front of me. For reasons I did not grasp he would probably have preferred to call the police, but at the same moment I heard my mother call out:

'Trond!' from further down the street, 'Trond! I can see it, it's here. The Wärmlandsbank is here!' she shouted, a bit louder than I thought was necessary. But luckily she had not cottoned on to what was happening in my life at my end of the street, and then I stepped out of the circle, the shining arrows stopped shining, and diagrams and lines melted away and ran down the gutter in a thin grey stream and vanished into the nearest drain. There were red marks from my nails in my right palm, but the choice was made. If I had punched the man in Karlstad, my life would have been a different life, and I a different man. And it would be foolish to maintain, as so many men do, that it would have come to the same thing. It would not. I have been lucky. I have said that before. But it's true.

I didn't want to go into the bank, so I waited outside between the windows with one shoulder against the grey brick wall and my father's woollen scarf round my neck; October slapping my face, a clear feeling of the Klara river not far behind me and all that it carried with it, and a shiver in my stomach, as if I had been on a long run and had got my breath back, but the effort was still within me. A light someone had forgotten to put out.

My mother went into the bank with the authorisation from my father in her hand; defiant and ready to get the task accomplished, but also burdened with shyness about her Norwegian. She was gone for almost half an hour. Goddamn, it was so cold out there in the street, I was sure I was going to get sick. When my mother came out at last with a confused, almost dreamy expression on her face, I felt as if the chill from the river had laid a film of some unknown material round my body and made me a fraction more aloof, a fraction more thick-skinned than I had been before. I straightened up and said:

'How did it go in there? Could they not understand what you said, or wouldn't they give you any money? Or maybe there wasn't an account?'

'Oh, no,' she said. 'It all went smoothly. There was an account, and they gave me the money that was in it.' Then she laughed a little nervously and said:

'But there was only 150 kroner. I don't know, don't you think that seems very little? Of course I know nothing about it, but how much can you really make on timber like that, do you think?'

I was no expert about that at the age of fifteen, but no doubt it should have been ten times as much. Franz had never concealed the fact that log running was not done the way my father wanted to do it, that it was a desperate project, and the only reason he joined in to help was because they were friends, and he knew why my father was so desperate. And even though my father and I had freed a jam from those rapids before we had to turn back and I had to go home, that was not enough. The river must have put its brakes on quite mercilessly; the water level sinking at full speed to its normal level for July after the rainstorms, and the timber crashed and turned over and piled itself up in huge tangles that only dynamite could loosen when the time came, bored itself into stony banks or sunk pathetically to the bottom in the low water and had not budged, and only a tenth of the timber landed at the saw-mill before it was too late. And that for a price of no more than 150 Swedish kroner.

'I don't know,' I said. 'I don't know how much money you can make from timber. I have no idea.'

We stood on the pavement in front of the Wärmlandsbank looking at each other; I sullen and ungiving, as often I was towards her, and she confused and irresolute, but with no bitterness in her that day. She chewed her lip, suddenly smiled and said:

'Oh, well, we did have a day out together, you and I, that doesn't happen every day, does it?' And then she laughed. 'Do you know what the funniest thing is?'

'Is there anything funny?' I said.

'We have to use the money here. We're not allowed to take it into Norway just like that.' She laughed out loud. 'It's something to do with currency restrictions, which I ought to have known about, of course. I'm afraid I haven't paid close enough attention. I'll have to do that from now on, won't I?'

She really never did do that, she was too vague in her ways, too preoccupied with her own thoughts most of the time. But on that day she was all of a sudden wide awake. She laughed out loud again, grasped my shoulder and said:

'Come on. I want to show you something I saw on the way up.'

We walked down the street together towards the station.

I was not so cold now. My legs were stiff after standing still, and I was numb all over, but it felt better when we started to move.

We stopped at a clothes shop.

'Here it is,' she said, and pushed me in front of her into the shop. A man came from a room behind the counter and made a bow and was at our service. My mother smiled and said distinctly:

'We want a suit for this young man.' And of course it was not called a suit, it was called something quite different we had no means of guessing, but she parried it simply and with no embarrassment now; in a flash of elegance her heels clicked across the floor to where a row of suits were hanging, and she took one out and swung it round on the hanger and displayed it over her left arm and said:

'One like this, for my son there.' And she smiled and hung it up again, and the man smiled and bowed and measured me round the waist and from the crotch down and asked what size in shirts I took, something I had never thought about, but my mother had. Then he went over to the rail and took out a dark blue suit he thought would be the right size and pointed to a fitting room at the back of the shop, smiling all the while. I went into the cubicle and hung the suit on a peg and started to undress. There was a tall mirror there and a stool. It was so hot in the shop that the skin of my stomach started to prickle and it prickled down along my arms. I felt dizzy and drowsy and sat on the stool with my hands on my knees and my head in my hands. I had only my blue shirt on and my underpants and could easily have fallen asleep right there if my mother had not called:

'Are you alright in there, Trond?'

'Yes, I'm fine,' I called back, stood up and started to put the suit on; trousers first and then the jacket over the blue shirt. It was a perfect fit. I stood there looking at myself in the mirror. I bent down and put on my shoes and straightened up and looked at myself again. I looked like someone else. I buttoned the top two buttons of the jacket. I rubbed my eyes and my face with the backs of my hands, round and round, and ran my fingers hard back through my hair, many times, pushed the fringe to one side and the hair by my temples behind my ears. I rubbed my mouth with my fingertips, my lips were prickling, and the blood was prickling in my face, and I slapped my face several times. I looked in the mirror again. Peering and making my mouth tight. Turned to one side while I looked over my shoulder in the glass and did the same the other way. I looked a completely different person from the one I had been that day. I did not look like a boy at all. I combed my hair with my fingers several more times before going out into the shop, and I could swear my mother blushed when she saw me. She bit her lip quickly and went over to the man who was back in his place behind the counter, and she still walked briskly.

'We would like to have that one,' she said.

'That will be exactly ninety-eight kroner,' he said, and now he was smiling broadly.

I was still standing outside the cubicle. I saw my mother bending over the counter, I heard the sound of the till, and the man saying:

'Very many thanks, Madam.'

'Can I keep it on?' I said in a loud voice and they both turned and looked at me and nodded as one.

I had my old clothes in a paper bag, which I rolled up and carried under one arm. When we were out on the pavement and walked on down to the station and to a café, perhaps, for something to eat, my mother put her arm in mine, and we went on like that, arm in arm like a real couple, light on our feet, our heights a match, and she had a click in her heels that day that echoed from the walls on either side of the street. It was as if gravity was suspended. It was like dancing, I thought, although I had never danced in my whole life.

We were never to walk like that again. When we came home to Oslo, she fell back into her own weight and remained that way for the rest of her life. But on that day in Karlstad we walked arm in arm down the street. My new suit fitted my body so lightly and moved with me every step I took. The wind still came icily down between the houses from the river, and my hand felt swollen and sore where the nails had pierced the skin when I clenched it so hard, but all the same everything felt fine at that moment; the suit was fine, and the town was fine to walk in, along the cobblestone street, and we do decide for ourselves when it will hurt.